the pain in needles and whiskey, in babies that float, in the car on the highway with the windows down--maybe all at the same time, forever fleeing but never able. *MONARCH* is packed with troubles, richly drawn and wrenched from alleys, from mattresses, lest we forget. —**THEA SWANSON**, author of *Mars*

Simultaneously raw, ferocious, frank and tender, these stories take readers on a harrowing journey of self-discovery and loss. There is a brutal beauty in this book as again and again, Tobias' characters touch that throbbing desire to live and love dangerously. Emily Jon Tobias is merciless in this collection; her stories cut straight to the heart. This is unflinching prose at its best.
—**LEAH BAILLY, PH.D.**, author and educator, winner of 2022 *CRAFT* First Chapters Contest

MONARCH is a startling debut from a gifted, compassionate writer. Emily Jon Tobias's stories shock, awe, wound, and--ultimately--lift your heart. So many times will lives seem in ruin only to emerge more beautiful than before, not unlike a monarch butterfly shattering through its motley cocoon.
—**SARAH BALAKRISHNAN, PH.D.**, writer/scholar/editor, winner of *Narrative Magazine*'s Best Under 30 Prize for fiction

Libraries and readers seeking stories about addiction, transformation, success, and failure will find *MONARCH* captures a series of alterations and relationships that reflect love, loss, and the outer limits of the underbelly of American culture and influence. Highly recommended, this literary work will especially spark book club discussions of contemporary women's writings that are firmly rooted in emotional and social change.
—**D. DONOVAN**, Senior Reviewer, *Midwest Book Review*

The eleven stories in Emily Jon Tobias's collection entitled *MONARCH* are a true testament to the author's ability to elevate and elucidate for the reader what it truly means to be part of a marginalized, often forgotten community. Tobias uses a deftness of hand in all of the stories, taking the reader into the world of those who suffer the most with the least amount of attention. When I read the title story, "Monarch" I felt as if the author had a window into my soul. Any person who has ever experience abuse or microaggressions, will feel a tug towards this story and others in this collection. If the reader has somehow been fortunate enough to escape the heartbreak and neglect expressed in these stories, they can consider themselves lucky and they can thank Tobias for showing them an unflinching look into a world of pain but also a world of resilience. Tobias is only going to grow as an author and a truthteller. I count it an honor to witness a portion of her journey and I am buckling up my seatbelt for what is to come next.

—**ANGELA JACKSON-BROWN**, award-winning author of
When Stars Rain Down and *The Light Always Breaks*

With prose at once sparse and weighty, Tobias effortlessly embodies the styles of Denis Johnson and Raymond Carver--while making them all her own. In this impressive debut collection, Tobias casts the spotlight on a wide array of characters/(unsung antiheroes) from varying walks of this often bleak thing called life. Showing us a vast scope of seemingly tranche de vie scenarios, ranging from "Nova" to "Fish and Flowers," each tale of quiet woe in *MONARCH* offers its reader a kind of romantic fatalism, embedded among such philosophical themes as: the patriarch as fallen god ("Jesus Wears Bermudas"), abusive relationships and repression ("Red Cardboard Hearts Hanging From Strings") and being an addict flitting among the invisible great unwashed

("Under Her Cellophane Skin"). Wherever you fall on the spectrum of this existence, Tobias has surely covered it within these pages in delicate, thought-provoking detail.

—GENNA RIVIECCIO, Editor-in-Chief, *The Opiate* magazine

In Emily Jon Tobias's raw and stunning story collection, grief, longing, fear and addiction live as companions to adoration, survival and the holy. Tobias's characters are desperate and sorrowful, lost and grimly doomed—except in those moments when, as they frequently do, they soar. Here are characters who, like us, are broken and bruised: in ways that feel familiar and in ways that deeply unsettle. Longing for safety, for connection, they move through the world like cats in the night: on the hunt for some elusive sustaining force. Prowling the bitterest darkness, ravenous and unceasing, and also—in ways even they may not yet recognize—unexpectedly and uncompromisingly free.

—SHARI MACDONALD STRONG,
Editor of *The Maternal Is Political*

Tobias's debut collection of transformational stories evokes the pain and pleasure of self-acceptance after years of self-denial. Take the amazing ride of actualization with each of Tobias's characters as they evolve like monarch butterflies in this evocative collection.

—LISA KASTNER, Founder and Executive Editor
of Running Wild and RIZE Presses, and author
of the acclaimed lycanthrope novel, *CURE*

An emotionally poignant debut collection. Tobias fashions perspectives that feel both familiar and fresh. Her characters struggle with mental health, body image, addiction, lost relationships, and hurts that many of us will recognize, whether in ourselves or those around us. At the core, *MONARCH* is about connection, how we all seek it in some way or another, how we can find love in surprising ways, how our desire for love can also cause pain. Tobias's stories will leave your ears ringing, her characters' voices resonating like a song, swooping between heartache and soulful hope.

—J SALER DREES, *Flash Fiction Magazine* editor

Slipping inside the pages of *MONARCH* feels like hopping in a getaway car with Emily Jon Tobias, who rockets readers through richly-drawn landscapes where characters come to life in all their broken beauty. This collection is a powerful and unflinching exploration of the hunger we feel for love, acceptance, and ultimately, belonging. *MONARCH* sizzles with electric imagery that burns with neon brightness long after the final sentence. Some lines that leap off the page include: "On the meds, life is a wrist watch and she's the broken second hand, wound up but not going anywhere."; "For her father, trying to help his wife was like being outdoors during a tornado. He went underground too late, after she'd already blown through him." I'm eagerly awaiting Emily Jon Tobias's next work.

—LIZ ALTERMAN, author of *The Perfect Neighborhood*

Emily Jon Tobias is a bold and charismatic writer whose significant gift is connecting readers to her soulful life journey and empathic heart. In these rich, original, and emotionally compelling stories, she reveals complex and memorable characters and their contemporary challenges as a way of providing her fresh and rewarding perspectives on compassion, healing, and the enduring power of hope … and of love.

—JOE MAITA, Editor/Publisher, *Jerry Jazz Musician*

Emily Jon Tobias' beautiful and powerful words go straight to the hearts of her readers. She maintains the tension in her stories of damaged women through careful use of detail, metaphor, and point of view. Sometimes her characters struggle to help others, sometimes they punish themselves, and sometimes they seek revenge. Together these women make *MONARCH* a collection impossible to put down.

—**STEVE LINDAHL**, Managing Editor of
Flying South Literary Journal

Emily Jon Tobias sets us free by revealing that which shackles us. She takes us into the tight, uncomfortable holes of our humanity and gives us space to consider what damage might get done and allows us to emerge through the opening into what she sees beyond. Taking on the gritty bits without flinching, Tobias writes to those of us who believe we can't be saved by reminding us that making mistakes is not the same as being one.

—**COURTNEY MORGAN**, President of *Talking River Review*

In this collection of portraits, Tobias explores the unsettling beauty to be found in the places where dark and light dwell together. These stories do not shy away from the depths, as though mining the source of feminine healing to lead us fearlessly and unashamedly forward.　　　　—**JENNIFER TOP**, TulipTree Publishing

MONARCH

MONARCH

STORIES

EMILY JON TOBIAS

BLACK LAWRENCE PRESS

Black
Lawrence
Press

www.blacklawrence.com

Executive Editor: Diane Goettel
Book and Cover Design: Zoe Norvell

In June of 2023, Black Lawrence Press welcomed numerous existing and
forthcoming Nomadic Press titles to our catalogue. The book that you hold in
your hand is one of the forthcoming Nomadic Press titles that we acquired.

Published 2024 by Black Lawrence Press.
Printed in the United States.

This book is dedicated to my mother,
who taught me that how I love makes me who I am.

Thank you for being my safest place to land.

Table of Contents

FOREWORD

Every now and again a writer comes along with an unerring ear for story pitch—a kind of instinctual understanding of nuance, grit, shift, tilt, tone, tenor, atmosphere, and lyricism. Couple that with a searing vulnerability, a deep empathy for the characters and the flawed, urgent, and tender lives they live in unforgiving but balanced and well-developed worlds as they struggle to reclaim loss and dignity and against seemingly impossible odds. A belief that all things can be turned toward an uneasy yet earned grace and an unsentimental redemption. Add all this together, and you have Emily Jon Tobias.

These stories enact the structures of the narratives they pursue, from the origami-like folds and turns in "Red Cardboard Hearts Hanging from Strings," to the burning heart of the center of the story, "Nova," to the grandeur and yet gentle spread of "Monarch" and so many others. It is clear this writer has worked hard to give each story its own craft, its own drive, and its uniqueness, and so well has this been done that no story feels the same as any other— you can feel the capacious imagination and elegant language of Emily throughout the collection, but each story surprises the reader in its turns and twists.

This remarkable debut collection traverses many of the parts of America that are unseen, or at least, unseen in this way, and gives us a wealth of material to engage with and themes that make a collection worth biting into—loyalty, betrayal, happiness and deep sorrow, addiction and victory, and a reclamation of selves against the nearly impossible grind of modern American life.

You are never the same as a reader once you spend time in Emily's work. You come out changed for the better; more compassionate, more tender even, embraced perhaps, but in all cases, with an unshakable belief that good art, good storytelling, like a good country or blues song, can be a road map to a better place.

—CHRIS ABANI,
author of *The Secret History of Las Vegas*

INTRODUCTION

My mom raised me as a Midwesterner in an ordinary, middle-class American suburb where, as a kid, along with being a poet, the only dream I had was being on the road. I left home young, yearning for a sense of belonging. Live music became my road map through America, and I exchanged my family for friends on its streets. I became intoxicated by all our states, carved into the concrete of this country by how hard I danced here. I got high too many times. Open highways felt more like home than any one place I called my own. But a crack in me was forming, a deep chasm, knowing that one day, I'd have to come down.

Throughout my life, average abuses and abandonments happened, traumas no more or less severe than anyone else's. Some were subtle, shifted in the wind like supple reeds. Others were deep, etched and scarring. While dark nights fell against the landscape of America, sunrises became harder to bear. Addictions took root like weeds. I became hard as cement, obsessions alive and vining, choked around my neck. Pain turned to rage as wounds festered. I became the abuser, prey turned predator. I hurt others. I left. Then later, the knife turned inward, hurt to be reborn as shame. Still fleeing at forty, I jumped my last train headed for a final wreck. I had betrayed myself over and over again. I was dying, no more than a shell, cracked.

On October 10, 2015 in a Seattle rehab, I was reminded of an old Leonard Cohen song, and I realized, finally, through my cracks, a little light had gotten in. On the road to recovery since, I have often idled at the stoplight long enough to glance in the rearview at the woman I was, now almost unrecognizable. Today, my spirit revs to go beyond the crossing, to go forward. In the light of reflection, I realize that I am not the woman I used to be.

I offer the stories in *MONARCH* to honor each human being's capacity for change. Characters drive this collection, which amplifies the stories of unsung heroes who are shades of the sufferers and healers in all. Together, the stories in *MONARCH* explore the human condition through the lens of wounded warriors who learn to love by giving and receiving small acts of kindness. *MONARCH*'s characters bear traumas with their bodies, and often, they transgress. America's city scars, sewers, alleyways, and bars are landscape to their wars, as characters heal and transform under wind turbines and on open roads, in golden cornfields and with the wails of Chicago blues. They break in, break down, and ultimately, break open.

An inclusive invitation, *MONARCH* aims at an intimate portrayal of scarred characters on American streets beating the drum of current culture against the fierce rhythm of critical social justice issues. My hope is that readers are compelled to traverse these territories rather than flee. If willing to embark, I hope readers will feel safe to emote, to open their hearts to the ravaged, littered bits of us who despair and long for love. *MONARCH*'s mirror reflects a changed view of America's corners, where compassion shines even in the darkest hours, and I hope readers can find themselves there. So that when the trip is over, kindness compels us onward.

In the spirit of *MONARCH*'s transformation, may those who have felt abandoned be held; may those who have been ignored feel heard; may those who have remained unseen become emboldened. With this, I urge all to enter these pages with an open heart, where love ultimately reigns and light shines when it's time to break.

RED CARDBOARD HEARTS
HANGING FROM STRINGS

HE'D BEEN CLEAR with you early on that having a family was never part of his game plan. You'd assumed he'd change his mind when he married you in a King County courthouse that stormy Thursday in February. You wore a black dress, forgetting about the holiday altogether. No bouquet, no corsage, not even a rose tucked behind your ear. Why? Because I'm allergic, Liza, fuck. How many times do I have to say it?

He was angry with you on the drive to the courthouse. Half-drunk—you only realized it because of how hard he gripped the wheel when you touched his arm. He said nothing. You lit a cigarette. He locked your window, leaving you to ash in your hand. Can you put this out, please? you asked. He looked straight ahead, mouth turned down. Baby, please? you begged, mouth forced up at the corners. You handed over the burning filter. He rolled down your window and flicked the butt out your side. You leaned back just in time, watching the thing get taken by the wind and rain. He took a long, deep breath before hitting the child lock on his side, securing your side of the car.

You sat together, waiting behind the bar in the gallery of the courtroom while an older couple finished their ceremony. The woman wore a long, flowered dress. She was taller than her man, with bright feathers in her hair. She reminded you of a peacock. She held a young girl's hand while the judge read the vows. You heard them kiss from where you waited. The woman was weepy but gleaming, and she kept touching the side of the man's face with a tissue while tears rolled down hers. They were smiling, especially the daughter, and all three huddled at the end. The girl walked out between the couple, each hand in one of theirs. When the door closed behind them, the air thickened as if in a vault. Your left leg began to tremble.

Two weeks before, you'd lost the baby. The pregnancy was no shock given that you'd stopped taking your birth control pills after a conversation with your mother that ended something like,

When are you going to grow up, Liza?

Maybe never, Mother.

What else, Liza. *What else?*

What else is there, Mother?

Then, one Thursday night, he held up a small baggie, swaying it back and forth. After the first line, he ran his hand along your thigh. You sucked salt off the backs of each other's hands and clinked wine glasses of cheap tequila together until one shattered, leaving you holding just the jagged stem, as if in ritual. Liquor ran down your hand, your wrist, your arm. Like you, standing there, too high, on one last sundown of Hanukkah in your childhood home. The only teenage marking left on your body, a hot pink stripe against dark curly hair. You'd rushed home late from the 8-Bit Arcade, barely making it on time, your mother already in position at the dining room table. She loomed like a vintage portrait on the wall in the murky light from that ancient stained-glass chandelier. *Barukh ata Adonai,* you sang and lit the match ... *Eloheinu melekh ha'olam* ... the candle shifted ... you reached to catch the menorah from falling, your sleeve inching up. When your mother saw the small crane tattooed on your inner wrist, she kept her eyes down and said, Disgraceful. That was *all* she said. Then she left you standing there with wax dripping down your hand.

Later that night, he grabbed the bottle and flipped the lights off in the house. Then he led you outside to his front porch, where you sat on the stairs in the dark, slightly apart from one another but angled in, knees touching. Your clouded head streaked the skyline into a million thrashing comets. He pointed to the giant Ferris wheel. Said he'd propose up there, at the top. I'll throw a penny in the Sound for good luck. No shit, you'll say yes before the thing hits the water, he said. You laughed and kissed him, tugging on the back of his hair. He pulled his face away and said, If you're lucky, maybe I'll even put a baby in you by winter. You downed shots after each empty promise as if in sport. By the end of the bottle, you were puddled on the porch, fused into one another. It had been decided: yes, he'd stay with you forever; yes, he'd prove it; yes, he better; yes, you would. Then you went back inside, to his bed, more rigid than before. When a bright sun broke like a yolk behind Pier 66, you two were still wide awake, then hiding your eyes from one another. Somehow you knew there was a little girl in you.

You tried to tell him, you did. But that way he looked at you ... the words were like dry bread stuck in your throat. If you could just get him to the courthouse, you'd tell him after the ceremony, you decided. Yes, right away, while he still had an oath on his tongue.

You'd already named the little girl Rose. And there she was, your child, in a puddle of your blood like a pistil wrapped in red petals. When you cried, salt from your tears spread dark on the bed. You bundled the sheets in your arms before your wound soaked through to the mattress, then dropped them into the washing machine before he could see. When he left that morning, you took a cab to the nearest Planned Parenthood.

How are you sleeping these days? the doctor asked.

Fine. Normal, you said. (Hardly at all.)

Lay back. Let me take a look. Just relax, she said, while you spread your legs, each foot in a stirrup.

Right, you said. (Impossible.)

Any undue stress at home?

You crawl your behind back a few inches on the table, still bruised from rough sex on a tipsy (blacked out) Saturday afternoon. Not really, you said. (Fingerprint bruises on your upper arms from that time you were in his seat when the game started … that welt from a playful snap of the bra when you took his fat joke too seriously … shocked by the first slap to your face in his car when you were too drunk at daytime … at a stoplight, in broad daylight, on the edge of Occidental Park where a homeless lady selling roses out of a bucket watched. You remember how sad the lady seemed.)

What about alcohol use? the doctor asked.

No more than usual. (Chardonnay with a splash of OJ over ice for breakfast daily.)

Sitting up, you tugged on the hospital gown to cover your legs. Any halfwit would've seen the signs. You never did. The doctor removed her latex gloves as if you were her science project. You left her office with a Valium prescription and a referral to her psycho-therapist of choice, specializing in addiction.

Give him a call, she said. He might be able to help you. In the meantime, try to get some rest. If you ever want to carry full-term, you'll have to slow your roll. The good news is you're young. You still have time. She winked and forced a grin, tossing her gloves in the bin on the way out the door.

You checked the clock on the courthouse wall. The second hand ticked. A court reporter dressed in pink filed her nails. She batted eyelashes at the oversized bailiff as he ducked under red cardboard hearts hanging from strings. Your phone rang. Your mother? *Shit.* Now? You hadn't told her yet. About the marriage. Not after the last chat. You declined the call quickly, stuffed the phone into your pocket, and there it was. There *she* was. Helena.

You ached for her, even years later, as if somehow she'd arranged the whole courthouse thing, decorations and all. Mystified, you asked around. Turns out, decorating was standard courtroom pro-cedure for all the lovebirds marrying on Valentine's Day. Just a little something festive to sweeten the big day, the clerk said. You shud-dered and kept your hand over her note in your pocket. How odd that you'd remembered to bring it, like you needed to take her with you over the threshold with him. That note she'd passed to you from under her desk in the fifth grade while Mrs. Furlong's back was to the class.

Take it, Helena whispered, just take it, quick. No, I can't, we're gonna get caught, you mouthed, shaking your head. The paper crane sailed off her fingers, gliding to a stop at your feet. Before the teacher turned toward her class, you had the bird nesting in your cupped hands on your lap. Perfect and delicate. Open it, Helena signaled. Inside, she'd written her name in penciled cursive along the edge of the bird's wing—*Love, Helena Rose Halprin*. You folded it back up with just the tips of your fingers as the scent of spearmint rode in on a breeze from the open classroom window.

Then, in the courthouse, you suddenly smelled her everywhere—the girl you finally put your clumsy mouth against in seventh grade, folded on top of each other behind the wooden slats of your bedroom closet after school one day. Light showered Helena's earlobe, her shoulder, her bare chest where a gold Star of David hung. You breathed into her ear as if fogging up a window. Like this? you asked. I think so, yes, she said, that's good. Neither of you knew your way. You fumbled with the button of her jeans and slid your wet palm under her shirt, and you thought you might be loved when her pulse beat into your palm against her back. Smiling in the dark, you swore there was just one of you.

She was supposed to be helping you study the Torah that day. Your mother had arranged it. That Helena, wasn't she beautiful up there reading the *haftarah*, Liza? You could really learn something from her, she said.

When she found you, your mother didn't bust through that door, no, she crept in, quietly. She stared at Helena's chest where the star was. You prayed Helena's faith would redeem her. It never did. Indecent, your mother said. That was *all* she said. Then she turned around, leaving you two standing there trying to cover yourselves, then each other. Helena cried. Then she left too, which just left you, weeks before your own bat mitzvah when you were to become a real woman. Alone, red in the face. Turns out, Jet, the family dog, had led your mother right to the closet, following the crumbs off a plate of coconut macaroons you'd carried to your room. You wanted to kill that fucking dog.

She'd never speak a word about how she discovered you. Your mother. Weeks later, you stood on the stage of the synagogue, shaking. The room was silent except for Rabbi Rosen breathing hard through his nose next to you. You looked for your mother in the front row while uncurling the Torah. Before your eyes could meet, your mother turned hers down and away. Her voice trembled when she forced her blessings while cold sweat rolled down your temples and the small of your back.

He nudged you with his elbow. What's wrong with you, Liza? Jesus, pay attention, we're up, he said. The whole marriage ceremony was already late getting started. Vows were forced, read like the end of some commercial for prescription drugs. When the judge pronounced you man and wife, there you stood, reaching back into your pocket while secretly wishing he'd eventually cave and want to raise some kids. He never did.

Some Tuesday in November, you'd seen him at a trendy spot on Queen Anne where *Cocktails and Conversation* was advertised across an A-frame sidewalk sign. Rain had smudged the *Conversation* bit leaving the whole thing questionable. Your two remaining girlfriends ordered a cocktail each and closed out their tabs.

There's a cute guy over there, you'd said, pointing him out with a subtle nod.

Come on, Liza, who are you kidding? Sonia said.

What's that supposed to mean? you asked.

Tash rolled her eyes. Your life would get a lot less reckless if you just came out of that fucking closet you're in, she said.

If your mother had been there, she would've said the same

thing with her eyes only. You imagined it would be that same cast down look she'd had that day when she'd come home early from work unexpectedly. And there you were, fifteen, smoking a cigarette under the garage overhang in a rainstorm, while Bill Braxton probably waited pantsless and shivering inside after he'd taken your virginity. You'd skipped school to share a joint with him first, and when you kissed him, he tasted like bubblegum. Let's do it at my place, you'd said. He resisted until your hands were down his pants.

You weren't surprised when your mother rolled down the driveway midday. Shameful, she'd said. That was *all* she said. Then, she sort of whimpered like a scolded puppy. You thanked God it wasn't Helena again and smoked your cigarette down to the end. By the time you went back inside, Bill was gone, and your mother was shut up in her bedroom.

At the bar, your two remaining girlfriends went home before the hour was up. You ordered another drink, tried to look busy on your phone. A woman at a far table ran her finger around the rim of a martini glass; touched along a sharp collarbone to check her buttons; pleated a cloth napkin, gently, to set lengthwise across her bare knees. Beyond her, he lingered at the bar. You spotted him again resting on an elbow with cuffs undone and sleeves rolled, leaning into his hip, like some kind of detective. He loosened his tie and unbuttoned his collar, shoving the tiny straw to the side of his glass to take a full drink from the rim. He sucked on an ice cube, then bit down. You watched him down his drink, how he crumpled the paper napkin and tossed it on the bar.

There was no first date. In fact, you skipped the whole dating phase altogether. After the second night out, you followed him back to his place. West Seattle, overlooking the city from a direction that disoriented you. He insisted you not face him when he spun you around and bent you over the living room furniture. With one hand on your nape, he angled you face down, your bare backside in the air toward him. He bound your hands in one of his behind you, fisting your hair with the other. His phone rang then, right when he was just about inside you. He paid no attention to the call. You saw his face reflected in the front window. He looked determined, focused, as if working out a puzzle, jamming pieces where they didn't belong.

You awoke in his bed the next morning, your tongue furred like a cat's. Your body ached. Shower running. Was he in it? You lifted the silk sheet to determine how far the night had gone. Bra intact and clasped, one breast spilling out the right cup. When you touched along your hipline, an image of your mother sprang up like a jack-in-the-box at the absence of your underwear. *Fuck.* Pillow clasped to your front, you kicked your feet wild, as if drowning. Finally, there it was, your thong, stuck like a dryer sheet in a ball at the bottom of the bed. Hooked by your big toe, you slipped it on before the water turned off, as if he'd be shocked to find you wanton.

Dizzy holiday months went on like this, your hangovers like skid marks on an otherwise romantic Sunday drive. Your two remaining girlfriends stopped calling, making things much easier on you. You'd grown weary of pretending. In the early days, you'd walk him to his office on Third Avenue in the mornings; head pounding, still slick with sleep and sex, him, clean-shaven, smelling of musk, just to kiss him out from under the umbrella and wait to see him again. Then, you'd stop home during the day to feed your cat, conversing with the feline about how well you thought things were going with the man.

One of these mornings he said, I will take care of you forever.

You believed him. Move in with me, he said. I want to keep my eyes on you. You thought about calling your mother, right then and there, to tell her the good news. Maybe she'd be pleased by a man choosing you. You never did. Instead, you tilted your head down shyly and slid your hand into his back pants pocket to warm your fingers. He held the umbrella, belting you down with his husky arm while you wedged yourself under his armpit.

Eventually, you'd forgotten to feed your cat for almost a week. No matter. As it turned out, the man required you to abandon the animal at the humane society before he'd allow you to move into his place. Small price to pay to be looked after like that.

On the Monday morning of your first anniversary, you wake after he's gone to work. For a moment, you wonder if you're still dreaming when you lie back with a vision of you and Helena in a car filled with rose blossoms. She drives ahead, you glance behind. A baby seat, strapped in, empty. In the rearview window, a sign says *Baby On Board*. You bring your hand softly to your belly and open your eyes. You've skipped a period. It's then you know for certain.

In the bathroom, you open the vanity drawer to find your script of Valium. One left. Next to that, your birth control. One missing. *Holy shit*. You look in the mirror. Cup one breast in each hand and bring them close, darkened nipples against your fair chest. You return both sets of pills to the drawer without opening either.

You move back to the bedroom, sit heavy on the edge of the bed, head in your hands. The air is dense and you are still. The last time you saw her was before all of this. You drove her from the city to her mother's house in Ellensburg. She said she needed to get out of Seattle for a while. You took the long way. She opened her window, all the way down, bare feet resting on the outside rearview, top half of her stretched across the console. With her head on your lap, you looked down to see her. It was sometime in July, yes, you remembered that endlessness of blue sky. She sang that one song you both loved, Led Zeppelin, off-key, low, like at midnight, when you'd get high with her under the stars. When you were both younger.

You passed a wind farm on the way. White wings of turbines stood completely still like paper airplanes at the tip of a finger. You found some agricultural road off the highway and made a quick turn. You stopped the car in the middle of the field and laid a blanket from your trunk on the ground. Topped by one turbine's giant wing, she made love to you there, and after, you cried as if you were visiting a foreign country on an old visa. An almanac of where you'd been together marked in the creases of your neck, written in the small folds between your thighs, hidden in the vestal spaces behind your ears. Each kiss a stamp on the landscape of your belly, each touch mapped out undiscovered land. She'd been moving on, concealing more and more of where you'd been together, waving you through the line. You sensed that this would be the very last time.

When you finally arrived at her mother's home, you waited with the car running while she waved to you from the front door. Helena's mother took her daughter into open arms, hugged all of her tight. Then, they turned their backs and headed into the house, still wrapped around one another. You waited until the door was shut, hoping they'd disappeared to the back rooms, before backing down the driveway.

You get up from the bed. Suddenly then, you yearn for your own mother. You'd say, Mother, I'm pregnant. (Indecent.) Mother, I'm scared. (Shameful.) Mother, I miss you. (Disgraceful.) You never did. Instead, you search drawers for something of his. You want to smell him, to be reminded of how angry he gets to show he cares. Like that musk of his you'd breathe in while between his legs. Or the smell of his spit on your upper lip after he'd leave you lying there alone. He was always sure to thank your mother because Jewish girls gave the best head. You go to the closet, rifle through his dirty hamper. You step inside. As if you will be the next one worn, you stand amongst his shirts. You close yourself in and crouch down in the dark. What's this? Something hard near your feet. You open the closet door for light and crawl out.

He'd hidden them from you all these years in an old box for his fancy shoes. Handfuls of letters from her. Each one perfect, still folded into a delicate paper crane, all tossed into a shoebox, as if fallen from the blades of those turbines on your last day with her. *I love you, Liza. I've always loved you*, in cursive down the spine of one; *Where are you, Liza?* in block letters on the wing of another; a simple red heart on the beak of yet one more. The last one you open says, *This is my last flight*, in small, careful writing and red ink. You touch each and every one with just the tips of your fingers. There is only one envelope crushed at the bottom of the box. You flatten the paper, gently smoothing out the wrinkles. In the upper left corner, in her own fluid writing—her address, still visible.

Quickly, you pack one small bag. You dump the shoebox of letters in, holding the envelope with her address in your hand. When your phone rings, you know it's him calling to check in on you. He'd want to make sure that you wouldn't be late for the dinner reservations he'd made for tonight. You watch the phone vibrate and ring. For a moment, you think of answering. You never do. Instead, you step outside into the open ocean air. A stray dog sniffs its way up your porch as if following a trail of crumbs. When the dog notices you standing there, he begins to pant, staring you down in the eyes.

You think he's smiling. Then he darts away toward the rocky shore. When the door closes behind you, you can still hear your phone ringing in the empty room, and you'll swear forever it was the saddest sound you'd ever heard.

NOVA

FIRST TIME I laid eyes on Jones, I didn't know how I would be tortured, gently, how I would come to rest just beneath her skin. The thing was never meant to be permanent. Me and Jones. Before her, I knew I wasn't built to stay. But here I am, inked. A stunted nail, the jailhouse hammer, nuzzled into the tracked crook of her left arm. We know what I am to her now, acutely.

I'd gone East LA to Santa Monica on the cheapest bus I found. Drank a pint nickeled off my newest foster brother some days before. I should've pinched it from the prick the way he'd always look at me like I was his very own blow-up sex doll. Off the bus, I walked, drunk, station to Venice Beach boardwalk. A lifeguard tower—Number 10, I still remember—graffitied with a pinup girl in a Darth Vader helmet smoking a joint, white bikini, one nipple out. Walls were neon, animated, surfaces and sidewalks all done up and painted like clowns, a whole stilted scene. Unnatural, really, artificial like plastic made to look like glass. Light flecked with spit and smoke came off the beach. A girl gathered cash in a hat on the ground from people wanting to pet the snake choked around her neck. One old guy, long hair, shirtless, had an electric plugged into an amp. I smelled cotton candy—sweetness on him—when he screamed *Voodoo Chile* at me. Over a low wall behind him, a rat. The guy's eyes were shaded, but I felt him watching me when he wailed. I kept my eyes down.

I found a cracked palm tree to lean against and crouched off the lip of a curb somewhere near the corner of Twenty-Fifth and Speedway. I lit a smoke and looked up. Green fronds reminded me of paradise in some kid's book. I squinted. Brittle at the ends, browning against blue. No one seemed to notice me there, some straggly thing like the tree I was up against. Nothing worth noticing.

I opened my eyes. Venice. Craned my neck, reaching for air. Gut rot from booze on an empty stomach. Looked down across my grass-stained front, wondering where the fuck I had fallen, sick, I swayed, and there he was again, front and center, like it was seventh grade all over again. The teacher who thought I was special. He said he wanted me. Young. My head all spun with clouds like blooms of chalk dust in the late autumn light of that classroom. I clamped my lids down and gouged at the hangnail on my right thumb, let ocean salt sting the raw flesh. A rock, kicked off the skateboard of some little local shit, made me flinch. So close, the ground rattled beneath my beat-up Converse as he flew by. Looked up, and there she was—big and noble—out of nowhere, like my mama's old ceramic Madonna: Jones.

Before I ever saw her, I caught a musky whiff of Jones off the afternoon Venice wind, like I was close enough to bury my face in the peach fuzz of her neck. I felt called to her like a cat. Catcalled. Busy rolling through the red light ahead—California stop—she didn't seem to see me. She occupied every inch of her very own matte black 1974 Chevy Nova, as she rode alongside a shotgunned no-namer. I braced myself and used the bandana in my Levi's butt pocket to clean the salt from my glasses, so I could see her.

The Nova rolled up, jammed to a full diagonal stop, front right tire bouncing off the curb, so close that, if I stood up, I could almost grab the plastic baby head superglued to the dash. Red paint across the doll's mouth caught my eye before the beefy rider did, and to this day, he remains nameless—a faceless object, thrown out way before the dried sage that sat propped against the frayed goat hide in the rear window.

She was savage, crude, as if sculpted from Venice sand, watered by its sea. Seemed she belonged to that turf since the beginning of time. I felt yanked, like I was downwind from some raw scent of hers. She was calm when she hissed, Get the fuck out, at her passenger. Then, she growled, Get the fuck out and don't look back as you go. What she held to his throat looked like a weapon clutched between her middle fingers. Now I know it was only the eagle talon pendant capped in steel, a thing she religiously wore on a rusty chain around her neck. The one some ex got her trying to win her back after she dumped his ass too. But the way she held it up to this guy's throat, with its point against his Adam's apple, it might as well have been a straight-edge.

With her free hand, she reached across his lap and opened the passenger door. He slipped up and out of the rider's seat, shuffled down the boardwalk with his tail between his legs. He dusted the Nova off his ass and shot me one quick glance over his shoulder. He gave a wave of his hand and said, She's all yours, then trudged toward the strip where he simply disappeared, swallowed up whole. Leaving just her and the Nova, right in time to swoop me off the edge.

The Nova's door hung open on rusted hinges. I peeled back from the palm tree like bark curling in the heat and staggered toward the car, then spread my hands across the Nova's roof to brace myself.

She leaned low-down across the seat, looking up at me, dark lashes and black holes of eyes.

What a fucking dog he was, she said. You, she said, like I was something worth noticing, get in.

Junkie Jones let go of the wheel, slid her bare legs across the hump to land in the passenger seat, leaving her shotgun seat empty. The Nova idled, gurgled a low, offbeat jazz tune. Then she was even closer to me.

Everything changed, like when it first gets in you, as I laid eyes on that tattooed wonderland of a woman. A bucking carousel horse wrapped around a pole etched down her spine, its mane draping along her shoulder and over the collarbone to her throat. Its bushy tail disappeared down her back into an unbuttoned waistband. Under the shredded hem of her cut-offs, a geisha. Blasphemy was scribbled on all her bends and creases. And a splash of color, like city neon in a rainstorm. Red puckered lips—a kiss to go with the FUCKYOU hacked on the underside of her soft wrist. A small, six-pointed star in the corner of her gorgeous left eye. One raven's feather spelled STRENGTH in blurry cursive along her arm. A hooded serpent with jeweled eyes and spiked fangs inside a thigh. Each ink touched another, a skin-thread tapestry that was Jones. I dug dirty nails into the palms of each hand, released and looked down at the crescent-shaped divots until red turned pale again. I wiped the corners of my mouth, wavered from the car and stood back, eye-to-eye with her, the hook, line, and sinker.

You drive, Jones said. I dragged long and hard on the end of my smoke, threw the butt down, snuffed it with a busted heel.

I tossed my bag to the back and settled into the Nova's driver seat, planting my hands on her oversized grungy wheel. I had only enough to survive. That bag was all I brought from the foster home.

I knew if I had slowed down to think, I wouldn't have had the balls to go. Somehow, I knew right then that Venice would be just one pad of many lilies strewn across my days on the road. Turns out, besides my bag, all the other shit just kept falling away each day to lighten my load for the leap.

I held my breath while Jones situated herself, moving aside cracked CD cases—Nirvana and Mazzy Star—kicking up feathers and sand from the floor. Jones had a thing for feathers. Wore one hanging off each ear from a steel hook that could catch a fish. She danced through the mess like she'd planned each move while I sat wanting to run.

From her seat, Jones looked me all over like syrup running down a stack, thick and slow.

What's your name, love? she asked.

Bettie, I said, soft.

You don't look like a Bettie, she said. My eyes shifted down, then straight ahead. Drive us along the coast, Bettie, I want to taste the ocean. Jones flipped the old knob and the radio buzzed from static to some oldies station where the songs all sounded like they were straight off vinyl. She turned it up and leaned her head back, like she hadn't rested in years. Took the aviators from the top of her head and sank them low across the slope of her nose.

I took the Pacific Coast Highway south. Visions of sunset in Mexico, un hibisco I'd pick off a tree overhanging a shared hammock just so I could tuck the stem behind her ear.

Jones sang low to the radio. Beach Boys' *Good Vibrations*. Don't you just *love* this *fucking* song, Bettie? She stuck her arm out the window, cupped her palm against the wind. I looked over and then she had her whole head out that damn window, cheeks ballooning with the chorus.

She came back into the car, turned the radio down a bit. You ever been banged on a Harley while riding backwards? she asked. I shook my head. One of my exes was a big, old motherfucker, all ego and attitude, belly and beard to boot. Tons of cash though. She reached toward her feet, came up with a spoon off the floorboard.

She laughed. Used to call me ARCO, after the gas station, cause that's where we met. I jumped on that bike and rode him ass backwards and sideways through the next few years. First ride on that Harley was at sixty mph down Speedway against the board-walk. Jones slid the bandana out of my back pocket. Held one end by her teeth, tied the other around her left arm.

I kept my gaze ahead. Next time I looked, she was drawing the rig out. Then she used one hand to grab hard on the sagging hill of her chest, the other on her crack below. As her arm fell limp to her lap, she said, That whole stretch has seen this treasure. It was sugary, the way she said it, slow-moving and tacky like drying tar. The spoon slipped from her fingers to the floor. She finger-flicked the memory westward, out the window, toward Venice's sea of salt, sand, and gypsy bruises. Gone.

Her head nodded and bounced off to the side, voice trailing right at the *good vibrations* part.

She was quiet. I turned the radio back up, sneaking glances at her as I drove. To me, it seemed the crinkle of her forehead told less of age than experience. Jones was barely covered, decked out in sheer, vintage rags, revealing her many sagas. Could I become one of her stories? Nothing was hidden from the eye, but something told me even back then that she was anything but loose with her nakedness. I could tell by how she wrapped her arm with my ban-dana after, like tending to a child's wound.

Hey, I patted her on the shoulder, you got any of that left for me?

She opened her eyes, looked at me above her shades. Then she said, If you're lucky, I will tell you the end of that story later. An omen. A curse? She paused, eyebrow cocked. She went on, If there is a later. For your ears only, promise. She winked, reached over, and dotted my nose.

I would discover there was always a price to be paid for Jones' attention. This time, the cost was a tantalizing wait.

We drove along the Venice boardwalk where misfits camouflaged seamlessly against ocean grays, stunted waves, and jagged horizons. It all blended together like God got bored and climaxed with one long stroke of a hand—a stretched out buildup, with a quick, smeared release. A sable sunset dimmed over lingering tourists and non-natives. I looked over at her again. I could smell the seediness on her. Jones slumped low in the Nova. Her body, spread thin, shellacked itself over the whole mess that was Venice and sealed it up. That place would never be itself without Jones, and she seemed to know it—that saintly mess with rings on every finger, and the way she balanced a Newport between her crooked front teeth ... she didn't just belong to Venice, no, she *ran* that place.

Bettie, pull over there, she said. I need to see my ocean. I drove her close to the boardwalk. She slinked out before I had the Nova in PARK.

I followed her down the boardwalk. She swayed, one long stride crossing over the next, hips moving in time with how the waves crashed. Feathers off her earlobes blew back, behind her. She outstretched her long arms, wrists twirling, fingers strumming ocean air like she knew just how to play the way the air moved her. When she spun toward me, Venice gently carried her hair forward, across her face, wrapped around her neck. She smiled. She smiled at me, then whirled back toward the water. I smelled her in the wind, vanilla and dirt. I breathed in. Venice. Sewers and smoke from good weed. Bodies and skin that had been there all day long, all along. I saw the old guy—from before—same spot, electric in hand swaying along to *Sweet Jane*. His shirt was on this time, he'd taken his glasses off. He looked at me again, but this time, I met his eyes and nodded my head. I knew then, he belonged there.

I looked for Jones. Couldn't tell where she ended and the shore began. I caught her feathers again, and she was like the black raven itself, swooped and circling. Sun settled. Tourists retreated. Venice rolled onto her back, into night, and all the shit came out of hiding, like fleas from a dog's belly. The place seemed inebriated. Against the boardwalk, Jones smoldered, and Venice flared with buzzed freaks like hungry flies. The tide bellowed behind them, and I heard an echo—a whisper in the rumble. An old familiar, like my mother's—*there is something mystical here*—and I was intoxicated, drunk on her voice, Venice. Hooked by the white fingertips of each capped wave tugging me closer. Venice breath was air to a fire inside me. All for her. *All for you, my queen!* I wanted to scream, overtaken by her untamed sea, waves wilder in dark than day.

Jones stepped onto the sand from the boardwalk. People swept toward her, into one another, gathering on the beach. I stood back. Seemed to me that Venice light didn't stand a chance against her midnight ocean lungs. I kissed the pads of my two fingers, then flattened my palm toward the shore. Jones was there to catch the kiss. She grabbed at the air, then waved me toward her. I ached, wanted to be snatched, taken. Venice and Jones—they collapsed me. I went forward, onto the beach, into her darkness.

When I walked up, two guys stood near Jones around a heap of newspapers and trash. One arranged kindling and a couple logs across the pile while the other set his boom box against a box of

Red Stripe. Jones was crouched, Zippo in hand. She lit her smoke, then the nearest McDonald's bag to start the fire. She leaned in and blew. Smoke from her dragon mouth made flames on the sand.

Play me a song, Skeet, Jones said. I want to dance.

Skeet tuned the box to some reggae station. Bob Marley. Good shit, he said, and lit a joint. She rose then—Jones—sidled toward me, blowing through the air. She became the *Natural Mystic* as she sang, commanding me with her song, and I did … I listened carefully so I could hear … I smelled her above the fire, through the wind. She had Skeet's coat around her, held together at her throat. Fire glow rose to meet her wings lifted like a phoenix. You cold, love? she said when she wrapped her arms around my shoulders, pulling me into the coat. My head rested at her collarbone where the tail of the tattooed horse would be. Skeet stayed to the side shivering, his face toward the water.

I'm good, I said into her chest. Never been better, I thought.

She pulled away from me, but we stayed touching. Skeet, joint, she said, then took it from his hand to balance between her lips. She ran her hands down the length of my arms, locked her hands around mine. We spun as one toward the sea. Full moon dangled way out there like a light bulb from some invisible chain. Scattered light gathered into a narrow strip down the beach, and we were on stage. We were the Venice stars, we were her night. We flew faster, dug our heels in closer, torsos leaning back, her hands securing my wrists, mine around her forearms. I was standing on the tracks, and Jones was my train blurred across the shore, smudged into Venice's papery waves. Her teeth shone against crests when she smiled, as the joint dropped from her lips. I caught X-rays of her in that light when she sang, like I could see right through her. We laughed. She stopped. I fell. We piled atop one another, rolling on the sand.

We walked back to the fire, arms locked. Skeet had a bottle in his hand.

Where's the other dude? Jones asked.

You don't remember his name, girl? Skeet laughed. He finished his beer. Threw the empty bottle in the fire. Ash kicked back. He opened another.

Should I?

I mean you fucked the guy. You might want to remember his name. Skeet laughed.

I fuck a lot of guys. Doesn't mean shit to me.

I didn't believe her. I imagined she was good at sex. But I didn't buy that she didn't care. She sat down next to the fire. Its glow turned her redder in the face.

He had to bounce. Looks like you ladies are stuck with me, Skeet said.

I stepped toward Skeet. You got beers for us? I asked. He handed me two. I opened one for Jones, walked it over to her. When she looked up at me then, I saw a snake in place of a dragon. She was shrunken. Her arms rested on her knees, head hanging between. I shoved the beer toward her.

Here, I said.

Can't.

Why not?

Feel sick.

Drink it.

Need something stronger. Quick.

You'll feel better if you drink it.

You got any cash?

Not shit.

Fuck.

She put her head back down. I set the bottle beside her. Stood up to face the water. Venice was coming closer, her tide rising toward our fire.

Let's go, I said to her. She didn't move. Skeet's jacket was still on the ground. I wanted to put it around her, to carry her out of there. I knew she needed something.

When I turned around, there was Skeet. Right in front of me, all up on me, not more than a foot away from my front. I stepped to the side to try to get around him. He moved with me.

Come on, man.

Let's dance, newcomer. You are new around here, remember. Fresh.

We're all set.

He moved toward me, but I ducked back toward the jacket. I grabbed it and stood up. Here, I said, take it.

Skeet took the jacket and tossed it toward Jones. It landed in a ball at her backside. She stayed still. Then, there was just me and him. He grabbed my shoulders and pulled me toward him. He lifted one leg. Wrapped it around my knees. Locked me in. He put his hand on the back of my head, lightly at first, pat, pat. Then stronger. He flattened my face into his chest. His palm was across my cheek, pushing, squeezing. He fisted my hair close to the scalp. Pulled back. My face was pointed toward that light bulb moon on a chain beyond the open holes of his nostrils, beyond the fire mirrored in his red eyes like a demon.

I felt her behind me. I knew she was there. Jones. I felt the coat around my shoulders. She had her hand over Skeet's against my head. She seemed to pry his fingers loose of my hair. He released. I fell back with my hand to my head. She took my place.

She moved her body against his, chanting Marley's *No Woman,*

No Cry while she tiptoed her fingers along his front, up to his face. Then she had her hands entwined with his, swaying, dancing. She pulled him closer. Turned away from him. She was facing me when she bent at the knees, still holding onto him, rubbing her whole backside along the length of him, down his legs to his feet, she crouched, leaning back into him, then snaked her way back up again. She did not lose my eyes.

Jones reached forward. Grabbed the bottle stuck in the sand from where she'd sat near the fire. She held it by its neck. Crack. Bottle against a burning log. She turned to him then, arm up. He pulled his face from the bottle, busted at the bottom. No cut needed. Just a threat. She dropped the glass in the sand. Then, she just looked at him, grinned, and said, There's more than one way to fuck a man.

Walking back to the Nova, I slipped my hands down the pocket of Skeet's jacket. Pulled back, and there was his wallet. When I passed it to Jones, she took the cash out and tossed the empty thing at me, high enough to catch. I missed. Bent down to grab it from the ground. When I stood up, she grabbed my face, pulled my lips toward her, and landed a quick kiss. The kiss was for the cash, not for me, not really. Shit had little to do with me back then, but I'd take it. Skeet's cash was enough for what came next. I tossed the rest of the wallet into the nearest bin, wiped my hands down the front of the coat, and threw it in.

I drove. She was getting sicker. Take me to my alley, Bettie. I want to share with my new girl, she said. Suddenly, I'd do anything just to be with her, to keep running. Jones's dirty parts made me feel cleaner somehow. My left finger twitched. I tried to cover it up by picking at the hangnail of my thumb. Blood trickled from my thumb to the knee of my Levi's.

A couple blocks up, behind Pacific, she said. You down, Bettie?

I'm down, I said. Without a doubt, I thought.

We chugged, rolled, slid in two blocks up the boardwalk. Stopped, idled. Jones's body hummed. Jiggled gently. Dumpster-sided back-alley business was so close I could spit at it.

Sun was on its way up. Beach light came off the ocean reflecting her face in the windshield. It was like seeing two faces of the same coin. Pallid was the one I noticed first; she was getting sicker by the second. I used the tip of my finger to draw a star in the fog on Nova's inside windshield. Jones's sour breath filled the car, and my mouth watered like the pang of cotton candy dissolving.

Best keep your hands on the wheel, she said, tapping the wheel twice, deliberate. You never know what can go down. She rolled her eyes and grinned. Then, she cupped her left hand over my white-knuckled right. She brushed along the side of my face, ran her finger down toward my mouth, barely grazing my bottom lip.

There he is, Jones said. Wait for me.

I'll keep my eye out, I said. Without a doubt, I thought.

She grabbed a wad of cash from her bag and backed her butt out of the Nova, never breaking the stare between us. Jones shut the Nova's door with a quiet smack. She swung her backside toward me and sauntered, full throttle, toward the alley.

I could make out a figure leaning by the dumpster—a small, hooded monster, thin and pointy. A dealer. He had her fix in his hand so, for now, he was safe. But only until she got it. My far-off view from the Nova was enough to see he was terrified by the blissful, awful sight of her. Who wouldn't be?

I took one hand off the Nova's wheel, flicked the stick to wipe salted sea fog from the windshield. A small scope, just enough clearing to catch them in my line of sight. I held the wheel tight.

A small clock on Jones's dash read 5:45. I ripped off a hangnail from my pinky. Smelled Old Spice out of nowhere like back then when it'd ooze from his sweat-stained pits under each fat arm planted on either side of me. I bit the fleshy part of my palm until it looked like a clam shell had burrowed there. I could take the car. Leave Jones and go. I wasn't born to burn like that, all ablaze and seen. I wiped the star from the windshield. Looked in the rearview, behind me.

Shit, I could've gone back, sure. I was scared to come out of hiding. I was scared of how good it felt to get found. But there was a flare inside me. A fire stronger than fear. Not back there, but within me. I looked ahead. I searched for Jones.

The dealer dangled a bag. She stepped toward him. They were closest at their waists. Jones still had the cash balled in her hand. Ran her fist up his middle. He caved. She had him. But then he pulled his hips back. Held the sack at the tip of her nose, carrot on a stick. He yanked back, grabbed her wrist. He held her face in one hand, squeezed her cheeks, put his mouth over hers. He pulled back still holding her puckered. He spat. She scrambled. He drew a small blade. He spun her around. Dragging his elbow wide, he cut her from jawline to hairline.

Jones fell bleeding at his feet. He stood over her with powder and cash in one fist, the knife in the other. He spit at her again, this time at the open wound on her face. Frozen in the car seat, I retched.

I sat straight, spine like a board. Yanking her bag to my lap, I dove in, rummaging fast. Empty-handed on the first dive. Just a wad of crusty, unused Band-Aids and a rusted nail clipper. Fuck. Looked around the Nova for something, *anything*. I fingered the cracks down the seats, no mind if I came up with a needle. I broke into a sweat. Wiped at my face. Finally, I spotted it. Must've fallen from her neck. That eagle talon hanging from its chain.

Venice swirled outside, but inside, the Nova was deadlocked, and I was still, hardly moving, barely breathing, and composed. A brilliantly aimed sharpshooter. I breathed in and blew Venice's grit from around the weapon's edges, still dangling from its chunky chain. I swallowed an iron mouthful, rusted and metallic, and armed myself. The claw's steel spike jutted between my fisted knuckles. I thrust the driver's door wide, left it hanging, and ran.

I ran hard. Caught up with him down the alley past where Jones lay cast off. Seemed he had forgotten the bloody mess he'd left lying in the alley. I swooped up behind him. Grabbing at his hood, I ripped down on him. I came from all sides, pierced him with the talon. I howled. Fanged his left ear and chomped, crunching on his lobe. His whine turned to a whimper. I bit harder. He crumpled, slumped forward, cupped a hand over his ear. But he did not scream.

Who *are* you? he said.

My chest heaved. He couldn't fathom a warrior armed only with Jones's adornment. He couldn't know that I was loaded with her power, or how invisible I'd been before. That for her, I'd become fearless, like magic. I was ignited.

Just go. Run, I said. He scattered.

I ran to Jones fiercer than I had arrived. I saw her all sick and sordid and for a moment, hated her weakness, beaten as I used to be. But even with a little hate mixed in, I loved Jones enough to wrap my arms around her wasted waistline, whisper, You're safe now. I put one arm around her hips, heaved her other arm over my shoulder. Her blood dripped onto my shoulder. Her feet dragged as I carried her but, together, we made it back to the shelter of the Nova.

We're going to have to get that stitched up, I said.

No hospitals.

I will be with you. The whole time.

She gave a nod like waving a white flag.

Early morning and already Venice had her chomp on people in line waiting to get fixed up at the nearest ER. Jones threaded her fingers through mine while we waited. By the time they came to get her, I didn't know which hand was hers or which was mine. They led Jones to the examining room. I couldn't stand to see her go. I looked around at the others, my head throbbing.

A man in the corner of the crowded room paced its border alongside me. He wiped his brow with a handkerchief, undid the top button of his shirt. His neck hung doughy over his collar. His speed picked up as he rubbed the top of his balding head. He stuffed his thumbs into his waist and yanked up, hard, the flicker of his wedding band hitting my eye. I rubbed my eyes. Was it him, the teacher? With his fat hand over mine, a ring finger dressed in gold, swiping virgin hair to the back of my ear, nudging his middle against my backside. I gripped the claw in my palm. The man talked to himself, louder, more frantic with each step, as he closed in on me. He was coming forward, closer. My ears rang. I gripped harder, felt the claw slice into my palm. Clamped my eyelids down. I sucked in my breath, chest puffed. When I peeked through one eye, he had already walked past me. I turned. He sat next to a woman, holding her hand. Emergency room. Tragedy, right. I caught my breath like I'd been held down under. My hand was bleeding.

I need a Band-Aid, I said to the ER attendant, and I need to see the woman I brought here. Is she almost done?

She'll be out in a minute. Just sit down and wait.

I sat on the other side of the waiting room. When Jones was released, I put my arms around her. Outside, the Nova cushioned Jones as I got behind the wheel. Venice's ebb and flow kept time as we sat silently, together. A parade of goosebumps clustered at the nape of my neck. One single tear swelled up in the dam of my left eye, and with it fell away an entire jungle of lizards, snakes, bugs, and starving beasts—fear released from its cage, freed to find a home outside of me. Jones turned to me, and with her crooked pointer finger, dabbed three stars across my forehead, then dotted the end of my nose.

There, she hushed, we are safe now. Safe. We would come to know each other's faces many times over, Jones and me. Safety and fear, together. When she said, I love you, even then, I knew she didn't mean it. Even then, being needed was enough.

With her touch, my heart swelled up so big that its lock pried loose and burst open. She came back to me again, and stayed. I was at the top of the mountain. All sand and sea and sky in one infinite moment. Later, I would anguish most in those moments, moments in which I wished I could yet again save her. Jones was to become my punishment, my crime, my penance. She was my savior before I saved her.

I came back into myself with only one thing to do. I punched Nova down Speedway, never alone, forever reclaimed.

MONARCH

TWO HUNDRED EIGHTY-FOUR pounds and counting. The scale creaks under the weight of Georgia's bulging thighs, trunk-like arms, abundant folds of flesh where lint and hair live. Her chins make for a blurry line of sight when she looks down, her toes barely visible beyond. She steps off the scale and wraps herself in the over-sized bathrobe. Gripping the sides of the sink to brace herself, she looks dead into the mirror. Good, she says into ocean eyes, it will finally fit.

That Frank is waiting in the next room, behind a closed door, gathers as a kind of pressure just below her left eye. A twitch, but nothing more. Georgia's accustomed to the weight of distance between them, the empty space.

Are you going to get dressed anytime in the next hour? The guys are meeting us for drinks at 6:00.

If you're in a rush, I can just meet you there, Georgia says.

In the next room, out of eyeshot of the woman, Frank picks at his clothes, impatient, calls out, Weren't you the one that wanted me to take you with this time? Jesus, Georgia, just put your fucking clothes on and let's go. She senses her husband's brusque hustle, pictures him huffing from off the bed as he shoves feet into his boots, stomps across the room toward the front door. She knows he always grabs a beer, pops the top off with an old opener attached to the wall under a hook holding his keys. This time's no different. With one swoop, he's got both in hand.

Oh, she can hear his temper rising, even from this distance, through the closed door. Still, she lets the robe unravel itself, opening down the front. Freed, her breasts roll down her ribcage, landing just above the belly button. She turns to the full-length mirror propped behind the scale, her stance widened. Her reflection spills over the mirror's edges so that she can't see her arms as the robe slides from her shoulders. She reaches down, pulling up on her belly so she can get a closer look at the curly hairs that weave around her crotch. Leaning in, she struggles to remember just how long it's been since she's been touched down there. *Too long to remember*, she thinks, and reaches in the cabinet for her Hershey's stash, hidden among the tampons.

Georgia, let's go, Frank yells from outside the door.

A twinge of cigarette smoke floats into the open bathroom window from outside where Frank is still waiting. She crinkles her nose, the corners of her mouth turning down. His smoke disgusts Georgia even more than the smell of the overcooked vegetables her mother had enforced in Georgia's youth. When the girl was nine, her mother decided they would diet together after finding Halloween candy that Georgia had retrieved from the trash bin outside stashed under her bed.

Georgia, her mother said, sit up. No slouching. I need to explain something to you.

The girl sat straight-backed on a tall stool in the middle of the kitchen while her mother talked, one hand to hip, a finger wagging in the girl's face. She explained what trouble Georgia had been for her during childbirth, how her birth was an excruciating labor of pain and tears that lasted forty-six hours because of the girl's nine pounds, eight ounces of baby body. That she'd suffered for weeks after, even months, while Georgia's father took over all household responsibilities. She went on about the depression, the devastating sadness of trying to connect with her tormented child. How bonding with the baby took real, concerted effort, like cramming for an exam. When the child wouldn't take her breast, the mother was expected to know all the answers. A forced bonding, her mother said, that turned her nipples raw and swollen, an attachment that almost killed her.

Georgia, your eating has gotten completely out of control, her mother warned.

I'm sorry, Mommy.

I will not allow for a complete letting go.

I will get skinny. I promise, Mommy.

I've worked too hard, suffered too much.

I will get ahold, Mommy.

That's right, child, we have *got* to get a grip.

Georgia left the kitchen that day grateful she hadn't killed her mother, more willing than ever to restrict herself. Soon after, the mother held her daughter's slack hand and led her into their fifth Weight Watchers meeting together. Georgia had learned how to fool the weight coach. When the woman's back was turned, she would shimmy her body to the outer edge of the scale and lift one leg just slightly, toes balancing above it, unnoticeable to her coach. This time, her scheme lost her a good five pounds when the scale settled. The coach was thrilled. Her mother high-fived the woman, gleaming, while Georgia stood aside, fidgeting with the zipper on her jacket.

We are all so proud of you, Georgia, the coach said. Her mother approached then with light in her eyes, a brightness Georgia had never seen before. The woman smiled wide. There was warmth around her when she got down on one knee to help zip the girl in. The mother tucked a strand of hair behind the girl's ear, patted her on the head. Then, she ran her hands down the front of the jacket, drawing it together around Georgia's mid. Too tight. Her mother tugged. Georgia blushed, sweat gathering on her nape. Her mother pulled harder. She stretched the fabric from back to front, trying to make it fit. When the woman realized she'd been duped, her mouth crumpled into a cutting frown. She snatched the girl by the wrist and dragged her to the car, forcing a smile at the room on the way out.

At home that night, Georgia cried when her mother forced her onto the scale. Proof of the girl's indulgence was on the table. She begged for the forgiveness of her sin. When the fork's steel tines rapped her knuckles, she watched the skin on her hands swell then shrink, puckering around each little wound. Maybe this will teach you the importance of limits, her mother said. Later, the stretch marks along her belly, her thighs, her biceps, all her undersides would remind her of those red welts. Tagged by the restraint she had always lacked.

In the bathroom, she still smells Frank smoking. Georgia's knuckles go white as she clenches her fists. Her body's an arsenal of anger, enough stored for a fallout shelter with full reserves, but the weight, the weight she carries in pain and pounds somehow softens her sorrow, consumes any energy left over for a fight. She releases her fists, watches her palms go red again.

Coming, I'm coming. Georgia pinches the white tag of a Kiss, peeling it slowly. The aluminum spreads back from around the melting piece. Her lips turn up into a soft grin. She sticks out her tongue to catch the Kiss off her fingers. The chocolate is so close to her mouth now, she can already taste it when, suddenly, it slips from her hand, plunging into the toilet below. Georgia heaves herself forward, shoves her arm into the water. No, no, no, she says, fishing the bowl. She swims her hand around in a futile attempt to recoup her lost candy until the water streaks brown.

As the chocolate dissolves, Georgia's heart pounds. She braces herself, both hands on the edges of the toilet seat. When she slides to her knees, her head comes forward, and a tear falls off her chin, released to join the waters beneath. She hears Frank's voice then, from way back when echoing against the rim of the toilet bowl. His voice, low and constrained, at midnight, after all the commotion was over. What the fuck happened, Georgia? Drenched, she stood before him while he sat on the edge of the bed, her jacket still zipped, elbows to knees, staring at his shoes. Wadded at his feet, the pamphlet from the doctor on postpartum depression.

October 10. Pacing the room, she told her husband what he needed to know, recounting the relevant details as if she were a confused witness to an unsolved case. Earlier, Georgia had clothed her child in a tiny pink swimsuit and T-shirt given to her by Frank's mother that said MAMA'S GIRL in bold block letters. To keep the child's hair from her face in the heat, she grabbed a bright pink silk scarf handed down from her mother. She'd worn it to her prom, when she had squeezed into the golden dress for a snapshot, praying to be queen for just one night. For God sakes, Georgia, suck it in, can't have you spilling all over the place for the shot. Turn to the right, so I can get your good angle. Don't breathe. Suck it in. Now smile, Georgia. One, two, three, say cheese. Her mother tied the bright pink silk scarf around Georgia's waistline like a sack of potatoes, the same bright pink silk scarf Ernesto Garcia had plucked at nervously to get up her golden dress later that night.

With the child at her hip, off they went, the bright pink bow bouncing with each step down the weathered wooden stairs, blue door left ajar. Rows of agave and succulents in rosettes lined the sloped sidewalk to Baby Beach. Late fall red spikes sprouted from their middles as the dead outer leaves gave way. Georgia looked past the neon birds of paradise, with their proud plumes and orange manes. She didn't catch the hummingbirds sucking on fuchsia trumpets or the tiny baby lizards eyeing her from the cracks in concrete. When the Monarchs swirled around her daughter's crown, she shooed them away, flipped her child from one side to the other. The child's bare feet dangled, one at Georgia's front, one at her back, as her tiny hand tightened around Georgia's clammy shirt, right at her mother's heart.

On the sands of Baby Beach, she sat cross-legged facing the water with her daughter in the cave between her knees. She wrapped her arms around the girl, felt jailed by the child, caged by her own misshapen post-partum body. Baby Beach with its confection of perfect sugary bodies—coveted, lovely bodies. Unrestricted bodies.

She scooped up her daughter, cradling her like an infant. Ocean foam crept over Georgia's toenails as she stood with the child in the cocoon of her arms, rocking back and forth, stepping into the swells. Hush, baby, hush, she whispered. Everything is going to be okay, baby. One foot in front of the other until the incoming tide reached her daughter's knees, and as the salt bath touched the bottom of the child's tiny pink swimsuit, the girl turned curiously silent, buoyant, lighter. Georgia unraveled her arms, placed one palm at the small of the child's back, the other at the nape of her neck. The water reached Georgia's waist, and the ocean floor turned from sand to rock.

Baby girl floated. Like an island over the hump of each wave until Georgia barely held her at all. Georgia's feet floated free of rock and sand, and the girl cooed, clouds reflecting in an ocean just like her mother's eyes. Georgia pinched the tip of the bright pink silk scarf that crested in a bow at the top of the girl's head, pulled it back—like peeling a Kiss—the bow unraveled into Georgia's hand, baring the child's forehead for Georgia to lean in with a kiss. Weightless.

Georgia told Frank how, later, the onlookers were full of pity more than shock. She could tell by the way they embraced one another, as if huddling around a campfire, eyes soft and drooping. She didn't question the authorities when they questioned her so little. It was clear they saw the disheveled, drenched look of her and believed she couldn't possibly be in her right mind. The rescue team spent more time asking her if she was certain she *had* a child than actually looking for the girl. When the EMT found her heart rate remarkably steady, Georgia pinched herself to get the blood flowing. She wanted to give the people the sorrow and fear they expected. Those crowds with their perfect sugary bodies came to soothe rather than scold, touching her back, shuffling around, offering drinks of water, a towel, a seat. Georgia tried to cry, to wither, to talk herself into the accident. And the truth of it was that Georgia didn't *quite* mean to let go all the way. But she certainly didn't mean to hold on either. She never intended to have to choose. Somehow, it seemed too fierce, too primal, to bear down on her daughter in those moments of weightlessness. In the end, the way she saw it, holding on was simply … unnecessary. It seemed to her that the sea could take care of them both, had a better handle on it than she ever could.

When she was finished, Georgia stood still. She stopped talking.

Looking to Frank, she held her breath, waiting for his reaction. He lifted his head, straightened his spine. We will never speak of this again, he said. Then, he stood up and walked out of the room past her, brushing his hand along her shoulder. That was the last intentional touch of kindness Georgia can remember.

Georgia stands. She flushes the toilet. Then, she unwraps another Kiss. Naked and loose, she devours the chocolate in one slurp, and with the sweetness lingering on her tongue, she hobbles toward the bathroom door, the last bits of sugar dissolving along with her moment of escape. She considers picking up the pace as she eyes the small safe collecting dust in the corner of their one room, second-floor, seaside apartment. After careful consideration, she decides to take her time.

In the closet, she can see the progression clearly. She runs her hand over the hangers of size-eight flowery sundresses, up in size for each year of the Gaining. Her fingers snag on skinny straps, pluck through wide-banded elastic polyesters, all in a nice row. Passing through time this way, Georgia catches the scent of her daughter caught in the folds of slimmer summer linens. Mornings, when the baby would tuck into her chest, Georgia breathed in the scent of new skin behind her tiny ear. She smelled like freshly baked cookie dough and plastic, sweet and clean. Once upon a time, before the Loss, all three of them lay together until noon on some Saturdays. Their rumbling bellies didn't matter, and Georgia craved nothing more than what she had at that very moment. Phone calls from family and friends were left unanswered. Back then, Frank could wrap his body around her, even as she wrapped hers around the baby, like he was the pod protecting its peas.

Georgia and Frank used to respect one another, before the Loss, before the agreed-upon silence and mutual loathing. For their first date, all those years back, he'd taken her for a picnic along the Pacific shore. He spread out a blanket for her on the shore, set out tropical fruits and fancy crackers with spreadable cheese on little paper cocktail plates. Then, he prepared the snacks, feeding them to her from his fingertips right to her mouth. When he said, You are gorgeous, Georgia, his voice was soft and easy as the roll of the sea.

Georgia, seriously, move your big ass. One more smoke, and I'm leaving, with or without you. Frank peers in through the window to check on her and lights another one. She knows he can't stand how slow she's become. Being able to control him with such little exertion is something she's come to enjoy. Her sloth eats at him, and Georgia certainly doesn't mind.

She finds the outfit at the very end of the rod, tucked into the far corner of the closet, still wrapped in a plastic garment bag from Dressbarn. She draws the dress from the closet with two fingers on the hanger's hook as if dangling rotten fruit, remembering her delight at how well it fit months ago in that dressing room with mirrors for every angle. She snips the red sale tag with a nail clipper, and $39.99 flutters to the carpet. She unzips the dress, holding it wide in front of her so she can step in. With both feet planted through the bottom, she gathers it up, pulls the dress around her middle. Finally, after some hard work, the straps balance on her shoulders landing the swooping neckline in place, just above the cavern of her cleavage. Fuchsia flowers turn light pink, stretched as they are against her widest parts, while the white beneath them holds thin and sheer. The bottom hem falls just above her dimpled knees, and as she pulls on the edge to make more space, she realizes that she won't be able to reach the zipper.

Frank, she calls out the open window, I need your help in here. By the time Frank is behind Georgia, she has put on the final touches, a bright pink silk scarf tied into a big bow at the crown of blond, messy curls. She looks like Shirley Temple in a fun-house mirror, everything so enlarged that Frank's head seems to be coming out of her shoulder at the neck, no body to be found. He treats Georgia like an overstuffed duffel bag, pressing her back fat in where the zipper is too tight. Skin catches in the zipper's teeth. He stalls for a breath to wipe away a small bead of blood with his thumb, then resumes, with force, to yank upward—stuffs, zips, stuffs, zips, until finally, there's a slack in tension and her upper back gives enough space for landing. He says he could have used a second man for the job.

Sick, Frank says, sweat beading at his brow. Just gross.

Georgia takes one last look in the mirror and cocks her head. Finds that she agrees in part with him, discovers she's also quite content with how much progress she's made. Georgia's body is, to her mind . . . fulsome. It reminds her of the way her name looks on paper, round with full G's and voluptuous vowels. Way before the Loss, when she was smaller, Georgia had often wished she had a name like Lilly. An upright, slender name, all I's and L's. A name like Lilly would suggest that she smelled nice and had a pretty feel to her while Georgia, on the other hand, made people think of a place full of sweat and fried food. Maybe that's been her problem from the beginning, why she always felt out of place. She never fit into her name. Until after the Loss, that is. Well into the Gaining came the understanding that her grief needed an entire sea, not some little puddle. No, Georgia's heart needed space to shatter, especially if she were to crack the safe gathering dust in the corner. The safe that stores the single leftover from the Loss, airtight and fireproof. The other effects of mourning are ingested—each Coca-Cola, a river runoff; every Kiss, a sprinkle of sand; each Twinkie, a life raft keeping her afloat. The way Georgia sees it, this is how she was always meant to be, given the way things turned out.

On the porch railing, a monarch hovers and lands. Instinct guides the small kaleidoscope to winter over in California warmth, but this one has traveled off course to deliver a message. Georgia misses the point as, eyes on Frank, she follows her husband down the weathered wooden stairs.

Georgia bobs along behind Frank down the street toward the corner bar. They walk, a smart choice given Frank's inclination to overdo it. The short jaunt leaves Georgia breathless and achy, so she lets distance gather between them. The farther away he gets, the easier Georgia breathes. A million tiny beads of sweat lubricate her limbs, but nearby, the ocean blows rich, soothing aromas, a breeze that wafts against large areas of bare skin left uncovered by her special dress. Georgia's mouth waters with the sting of salty air against chafed thighs. She enjoys the irritation. Since the Loss, Georgia covers herself, seeing no need to disturb others. The Gaining is to show the world how sorry she is, but the sensations her dress provides in this moment are so delicious, she can't help but feel content. Her heart slows, and between the thumps, she hears the silence after the crest of each tumbling wave.

Hey, you, want a ride?

Windblown surfers idle beside her in a topless Jeep. Georgia drops her handbag, startled. The youngsters, two young boys with two girls to match them, strike Georgia as simply glorious, half-clothed, bronzed and baked to perfection. She bends to retrieve her fallen bag, and as she stands, the skirt shimmies to just beneath her bottom.

The girls snicker, covering their mouths, while the driver continues, You look hot. You need a ride?

Georgia tugs down on her dress, considering her options. During the Gaining, Georgia has limited options, and, as a result, decision making has been made easier. She doesn't have to decide what to wear when nothing fits; she doesn't choose food when more is all that matters; doesn't worry about making Frank happy when nothing will. The Gaining keeps Georgia safe, enclosed.

Thank you for asking, but I'm due to meet my husband and his pals just down the street for drinks. He was walking with me, but I got behind.

One of the girls throws her head back in dramatics. Well, I wonder how that happened, she says.

I'm pretty slow.

I can see that.

All eyes are on Georgia. She reddens from the heat of standing still. Georgia understands this crew is sickened by her. She knows that their offer is a ruse.

The surfers jiggle in the rumbling Jeep, waiting for Georgia's response. Prince Charming reaches into a greasy McDonald's paper bag on the dash and stuffs a French fry into his mouth.

Want one? He grabs the bag and shoves it across his princess's lap toward Georgia. Or a handful?

How about the entire bag? I don't see the need for just one when it comes to fries, Georgia says.

Well, that's obvious.

Is it?

You're huge, don't you see that?

I do.

Don't you care what you look like? Charming's white wife-beater hugs his rippled abs, each muscle a sand dune that Georgia imagines his girlfriend ploughs. Georgia would rather knead his belly like dough, watch it stretch and spread.

The bigger, the better, she says, reaching for the bag, but the driver snatches it back. He balls it up, wringing out the brown paper soaked in grease, and hurls it at Georgia's face. Ketchup splatters across blond curls as the bag bounces off her forehead, landing at her feet. A humid eighty-seven December degrees has melted Georgia's makeup into pan-fried butter. Georgia looks down at the pile of fries at her feet.

Such a waste, she says, tonguing the salt on her lips.

We're out of here. Let's cruise. Tires screech as the princess waves like a queen while their ride folds into the road ahead.

What a mess, Georgia mumbles, brushing crumbs down her front.

She sighs. All the theatrics are a waste on her. Hostility is merely a formality. She knew what the Gaining would mean, even before the Loss, has known ever since childhood. Georgia's mother took her to Sears to buy her first training bra the summer before fifth grade. On the first day of school, Mrs. Ness assigned Georgia a front row seat, the straps of her training bra visible to the entire class through her white T-shirt. Georgia Porgia has boobs. Pass it on, whispered one kid to the next until Georgia felt their stares burning holes in her back. When Georgia came home after school that day in tears, her mother suggested a baked potato diet, all the rage in the early '80s. Maybe if you can just get a handle on this baby fat issue, Georgia, the kids will be friendlier. Georgia desperately wanted a handle, and to please her mother, so she decided to give it a try.

That was when she learned how to count calories. Two hundred seventy-nine calories per large potato, leaving enough calories for the six home-baked chocolate chip cookies she ate while hiding

in the TV room. The next day she ate only half a baked potato—
no butter—to make up for her cookie wrongdoing. The handling
worked. If she gave up a meal, she got a kiss on the lips from Danny
Boomer. Sacrificing food for a whole day meant he tongued her in
public rather than stuffed in the gymnasium broom closet. For the
high school prom, if she snorted enough to stay high and hungry
for two days, she won the crown, not for prom queen but at the
Burger King where Ernesto Garcia fondled her in the boy's bathroom stall as though he loved her.

Georgia bumbles toward a storefront business, leans in to use
the shop window as a mirror, knowing that at the very least, her lipstick needs touching up. In the warped reflection, even fingers and
elbows, her sharpest angles, seem more obtuse. She ruffles around
crusty ketchup to puff up her crown, rounding out the bow. With
L'Oréal in hand, she leans in face-first, close enough to fog the
window with her steamy breath. She shields her eyes to get a better
look inside.

Just beyond the glass there is row on row of home furnishings,
wicker sofas and plastic chairs, tables with lamps glued to the tops,
all made cheap by Asian children in a land far, far away from the
rich seaside town. Georgia puckers her red lips against the glass
leaving a mark she assumes no one will see. As she pulls back, a man
appears out of the void in the near distance. Dust balls hang from
his broom, and when he looks up, Georgia sees his face flash white
in the dark. He stalls a moment, then his hand raises, as if pulled by
a string, in something like a wave.

He mouths, Hello, how do you do? sculpting each syllable with
his mouth to make sure she understands. Yes, she thinks, a tidy man.
Neat in his clothes and steps, something exact about his manner—
fastidious, careful. Her culinary judgements are immediate. With a

starched shirt like that, this one must eat meals on a tight schedule. Oatmeal for breakfast at 8:30, carrots and bologna sandwich on white for lunch at 12:30, and spaghetti for dinner most nights, anywhere between 6:00 and 6:15 in the evening. Her hunch is that he's worn the same leather belt for decades, never gains, never loses. She doesn't realize how close she has come to the truth of this sparse man—his attention to detail, the rigor with which he lives his life. All she genuinely knows for the moment is that he is a pantomime window washer which she finds particularly silly, and in truth, quite endearing. He sticks up his pointer finger, crooks it toward the shop's front. She nods once, and he bolts toward the front where he waits with the door held open.

Well, hello there, he says. And your name is? His voice is deep, so full it doesn't suit him, much too loose and roomy for the scrawny man Georgia sees. She delights in his sound like creamy chocolate mousse—rich, airy.

The way he eyes her reminds Georgia of how kids watch cartoons—enchanted, eager, like she's the centerpiece of his smorgasbord. She wonders if this petite man wants to devour her. Would he let her dribble down his chin? He would have to wear a bib, which she presumes wouldn't suit him, although she's certain the mess would suit him less. She's right about how looking at her makes this man want to break all his own rules.

Georgia, she says.

How do you do, Georgia?

How?

Yes, *how*. He takes a step closer.

Perhaps you saw the French fry massacre from the other side of your window.

Only then, it seems, he notices the dried ketchup at her hairline, just above the right temple. I feel like I just stepped into a dream, he says.

Well, I suspect I just might have, too. Anything's possible.

I thought I recognized you from somewhere, the man says.

At the halfway point between them where their eyes meet, somewhere close to the bright pink bow atop Georgia's head, the air thickens. Something invisible is suspended between them—dense enough to ripple, light enough to float.

Walk with me, Georgia. The man reaches around the door, flips the OPEN sign to show CLOSED, and locks up. I'll take you wherever you need to be, he says, then offers an arm.

Georgia looks toward the bar. She thinks of Frank, the darkness inside, the low lights and grungy floor. Then, she looks up to the heavens. One cloud softens above her. The sky sweeps the wisp into the shape of an angel right before her eyes. Suddenly, she can't imagine being enclosed just yet. No, she craves winter winds off the tide. Today, she longs to be outside.

Georgia hooks her arm in the bend of his elbow as he ushers her down the street toward the bar. She feels lighter next to him, as if they're floating, with her body tucked under his wing. The palm trees they pass are dressed up as candy canes in Christmas lights, looking strangely misplaced in the afternoon sun and winter heat. They take the long way, strolling through the Lantern District, along Del Prado, window shopping. Georgia keeps her eyes down, relishing each step with this man beside her. They smile gently at each other when they pass the American flag staked outside the old hardware store as if remembering a shared, unspoken past.

Walking next to him, this stranger, this man with his small walk and clean smell, Georgia floats away from the sea of space.

On approaching Rita's Diner, he stops, turns to Georgia, and says, I have a feeling strawberry is your flavor. Let's go in and sit for a moment. He holds the door for her as she sets eyes on a corner booth. To make her more comfortable, he inches the table closer to his side. Turns out, they fit perfectly together, Georgia taking up exactly as much space as the man gives away.

When the waitress arrives, she doesn't miss a beat. Well, don't you two make a fine couple. What can I get you? She pops her gum and pulls out a pen buried in her brunette bun. No one is the wiser that he is a stranger to Georgia; she doesn't even know his name. Seemingly, he could care less.

We'll share the Kitchen Sink Sundae, please. He points to a photo in the diner menu.

You got it, honey. Good choice. She winks and swivels, leaving the lovebirds to wait, as he cups his hands over Georgia's resting on the table.

Before the Loss, Georgia had momentary surges like this, when her senses rose from the dead. Sometimes the baby's wailing shocked her back to life. On the rare mornings she mustered enough energy to rise from bed, she would wipe her eyes, surprised to find a full sink of crusty dishes and spiders nesting in corners. If the fog lifted long enough, she plugged the sink, ran warm, soapy water over the dishes, stopped it in time so the water wouldn't run over, and let them soak. She sprayed cleaner across the counter to kill trails of ants and watched them scramble to death before wiping them into her palm, sprinkling them like pepper into the trash. She tied the bulging trash bag at the top, pulled it loose from the can, and set it outside the front door of the apartment to take to the dumpster on the way out, with high hopes of making it that far.

Sitting with this man, she thinks back to the day of the Loss. How she'd found a sign written in her own handwriting, duct-taped to the front door of their apartment reminding her, *You missed your birthday*. The depression made her lose time, so she'd taken to leaving herself reminders of what she might miss. She flipped on the only lamp in the room propped on a stack of neglected books including titles like *Love Does* and *Love Wins*, yellow and wrinkled. Georgia followed the ripe stench of her daughter's dirty diaper to the baby's crib where the girl whimpered. Above the baby, a wall calendar hung alongside another reminder. This one in permanent marker, written directly on the wall in her own childlike cursive. *Stop being a shitty mother. Put the food down and take a walk.* She flipped from September to the next page of the calendar, ran her finger across the first row, and tapped on October 10. In the box, a sticky note was posted, *Now is the time.*

She stared at the child in her crib. The baby began to cry. Georgia lifted her, outstretched, then cradled her on her hip, more like a chimp than a child. While holding the child around the waist with one arm, she pushed the clunky old vacuum with the other, bouncing the child against her thigh to calm her. But the child only howled harder and harder, fighting with the roar of the vacuum— a cyclone of sound like thunder—crack.

Yank. Vacuum cord from the wall. Georgia sat the child on the floor, snot bubbling from her nose. At the top of each agonizing sob, she gagged, tiny cheeks blotched and veiny like the nose of a drunk. The mother began to panic when the child's nerves twitched and her fingers and toes stretched into webs. Circling the diapered girl on the carpet, Georgia broke into a sticky sweat. She ripped through her own hair with a brush, pulling it back at the nape. Fanning her face, Georgia paced. Hush, baby. No more crying, baby. Mommy's here, baby. Begging, Please, baby. When silence hit, Georgia thought it was over, but as soon as the girl caught her breath another wave of anguish broke, like a strong tow pulling the mother under until Georgia was drowning. Baby, baby, stop your crying, please baby, please, please. Georgia thrashed through the apartment, a tornado unearthing throwing anything soft and freestanding so as not to directly hurt the child. Unbreakables bounced off walls, pillows and forks and books and toys, windows yanked open, doors slammed shut, until all her hard housework was undone, until she stood, huffing and puffing, over the girl.

Stop being a shitty mother. Put the food down and take a walk. Now is the time.

She never told Frank. She was simply following the signs.

The waitress arrives with a tray balanced above her shoulder. On top, a Neapolitan heap drenched in chocolate sauce with a cloud of whipped cream floating on two big bananas and double cherries on top, all heaped in a mini metal kitchen sink complete with little pipes as feet, tiny handles that could really turn, and a faucet as big as Georgia's thumb. Two spoons balance on the basin's edges, one handle pointing toward Georgia, the other toward the man. He reaches around to Georgia's side and balances her spoon between his fingers. He plunges through the creamy top layer. gathering every flavor, slices through the banana, and scoops up a maraschino at the end for an Olympic gold landing. Georgia applauds; her ocean eyes narrow toward her nose, crossing at the luscious spoonful. Georgia's dimples twitch, and she opens in slow motion. His face flushes, his hand wobbles, a bumpy ride to Georgia's lips, leaving a dot of whipped cream like a cloud at the tip of her nose.

Oops, sorry for the turbulence, he chuckles and sets the spoon down on her side of the sink, holding the napkin he's lifted from his lap toward her.

Sugar pangs Georgia's jaw as she rolls the slick banana around like a snowball, gathering cream until her tongue numbs and teeth ache. She tightens her eyes to savor the moment. It's clear to Georgia that he is sweet on her, a foreign sensation since the Loss. This man's offer is tempting, Georgia must admit. Tempting, quite like his shop offerings: a blue light special, a bargain of attention, prices slashed so low, for a moment, Georgia thinks she can find a need for it, wonders if she can pass it up. For the first time since the Gaining began, she wonders if she should stop the suffering. She opens her eyes just as the last morsel melts away and pulls her hands out from under his.

What's wrong?

I don't even know your name.

You haven't asked.

I don't think I want to know, she admits.

Let's just finish our sundae. If you change your mind, just say the word.

It appears as if nothing seems to bother him, and Georgia considers this further proof that his offerings are bottom of the barrel. Georgia sets her spoon down. I didn't always look like this, she says.

No? How were you before?

Easier on the eyes.

I could watch you all day, no sweat.

That's not possible. I *know* how people see me.

Maybe you only *think* you know. People are like puzzles. They're meant to be confusing. In the end, it's just a guessing game that puts all the pieces together.

I wasn't expecting this. Georgia softens. They watch as the sundae turns soupy toward the sink's drain.

Who could expect this? he asks softly. Such a surprise, he whispers while his gaze seems to turn inward. Small surprises seem bigger in a life like mine, he says finally.

What kind of life is that?

I keep things simple.

I am not simple, she says.

That much I already know. I can see it in your eyes, he says.

He pays the bill, extending perfect courtesies to the waitress, hostess, cooks, patrons, and anyone else forgotten on their way out. As they resume their walk, she considers telling him how once upon a time, in a faraway land, there was a fork in the road. Back in a time before the Loss, before the Gaining, somewhere in between. How she knew that *Now is the time* because her calendar said October 10. How she had a plan to get a handle on her life again. How she cleaned the apartment for the first time in days while her daughter slept soundly on the bed, face up, to reduce risk. How for once she thought she felt a little better. But then her daughter woke and began to wail, and Georgia's flow was disrupted. The mother didn't have the right answers, she didn't know how to stop the baby's crying, how to ease the child from suffering. Offering her baby to the sea was how the mother could *save* her. And now this man sits before her. She has the strongest sense that he can somehow guard her, that he can somehow soothe her.

So, tell me mister, what *is* your name? she asks.

Gabriel, he says. Gabe Wade.

Gabriel Wade. Well, it was nice to meet you. Lovely, really, Georgia says, unthreading her arm from Gabe's elbow. This is our final destination.

So soon?

The truth is stuck in Georgia's throat like a tiny fish bone. She swallows hard to cram it down and steps away.

I'm afraid so, she says.

The woman stands at a distance, not guessing how much she has come to matter to him already, that this loss is enough to mangle him. But he takes it with a kind generosity, with grace. Nods his head. In that moment, he reminds her of when she first began to recognize that empty space where Frank's freedom and her isolation meet. The space where some couples hold hands. It's as if he, like Georgia, is resigned to being left behind. She notices the slump of his shoulders as his shadow leads him away.

Perhaps it's his chivalry, coating her insides like syrup, that moves her forward. Toward the coast. It occurs to her how late she is, maybe Frank will wonder, but the ocean's breadth charms her. Deep pummels of sound, then a gradual hush after each wave draws her closer to the edge.

The slanted route to Baby Beach hasn't changed much since the Loss, but she sees more than back then, when *Now is the time*. October 10. Now, with no child in hand, Georgia's able to take her shoes off and carry them. She looks beyond her feet, kicks a pebble with her bare toe. She watches it roll downhill past a mother jogging behind a fancy stroller, pushing the baby's chariot with such lightness and grace, Georgia swears she sees a smile on that mother's face. Georgia can't fathom it, a grin in the face of gravity, but sure enough, as they pass each other, the beaming mother's sweat smells like sweet perfume, her baby coos a light birdsong in tune with the mother's swift breath. Georgia squints at the shining town, looks around as if for the first time. specks of sunshine glitter off streetlights made to look like old-fashioned lanterns. A castle hovers over the edge of a high cliff in the distance, just one speckle against identical others, strewn together across rocky hills along the coast. It stretches out endless before her, nothing new, just that sameness. Her stomach turns like it did at the drain of the Kitchen Sink

Sundae with Gabe. Strappy palm trees bend top-heavy, sprouting from surrounding crags, suspended, like a trick. Threadbare skies hardly hold together, wisps of pastels beaten frothy then smeared across a hard blue canvas. There's something about the way natural light absorbs into the lamppost; how the ancient masonry suddenly seems pristine; and the way the glib mother glides by her, that fills her with the feeling that none of it, *none of it*, is real.

Above the castle, Georgia spots a bright pink helium balloon loosed above the glossy snow-globe town. As the balloon dwindles to a pin dot, Georgia inflates—brims to the thin rim of this fragile world. She rubs her eyes, thinks she's seeing things wrong, but there's no denying the rift of endless sea where land stops short at the shoreline. Baby Beach. Georgia opens her eyes. She searches the sea space for some sign of punishment—nothing. Just the constant sway of newborn waves mothered by the great expanse of sea. One single sound, the hiss of a sigh, is released in her exhale, as she heaves her weight, leaving footprints on the beach erased slower than she can walk away.

Hours later than expected, when Georgia finally enters the bar, she finds Frank in the middle of the dance floor, drunk and slumped around a pretty young woman, slurring to a sappy jukebox song by the Boss, Frank's favorite. Georgia pries him off the young miss, tossing Frank's arm around her shoulder to carry him home. On the way back, they pass Gabriel's shop and in the dim recesses, she sees he's sweeping out the far corner of the showroom. Georgia drags Frank up the weathered wooden stairs to their second-floor seaside apartment. When they reach the top, she says she could've used a second man for the job. She unlocks the door with Frank's keys, sets them on the hook beside the door, and dumps him on the bed.

Before disrobing, Georgia takes a moment to stand on the porch, to breathe fresh air under the moon. On the porch railing, she notices a lifeless monarch. *Left behind,* she thinks, and pinches its dead wings in her fingers, holds it up to the moonlight, and lets go. The majesty helicopters, swirled in gentle Pacific winds, landing on the ground below just after Georgia steps inside. She opens the latch of the small safe gathering dust in the corner with one hand, unties the bright pink silk bow at her crown with the other. Carefully, she coils the scarf in her palm, places it dead-center in the middle of the empty safe. She locks it up—fireproof and airtight— sheds her clothes and climbs naked into her bed next to Frank.

JESUS WEARS BERMUDAS

MIDLIFE, SHE'LL INCH slightly back from the barstool to drop her tube of red lipstick to the floor on purpose. When the Mister to her right hears the clang at their feet, he will pretend to be chivalrous by removing himself from his own stool to bend down to the sticky floor, so she won't have to. She will stall on purpose. As he swoops down like Superman, he'll gaze up her short skirt at her bareness. A flushed, pulsing look of desire will come over his face as their eyes meet. With his head between her knees, she will feel powerful, looking down on him. He will pass the lipstick up to her, as she takes his hand to guide him upright.

She will build a fleeting sexual affair with this married Mister under his assumption that she is submissive. She knows just how much power to withhold in order to make him explode with desire. Soon enough, the Mister will get hooked, like a fish flopping on a line. They all do. She'll get restless when enough time has passed for the sex to become routine. When he starts saying things like, *Maybe it's time we start talking about taking this thing to the next level*, she'll make her eyes watery by thinking of the few Misters she's ever really loved. She'll think of her father while she rests her head against the Mister's ribs. If she's desperate enough, she'll even think of Jesus himself. As the tears wet his tight abs, she'll rub him hard again. Her feigning will tap a wellspring of his arousal. He'll inch toward her unwittingly, like a tiny worm. If she can keep him coming, she's certain her crying will make him think she's falling. She wants him to offer up everything, just for the thrill of refusing him.

Next time, in a different motel room, he will have the talk with her about the thought he's having of leaving his wife. Idle words of atonement will become his tether. She'll pretend to enjoy sucking him off by moaning and making eye contact. By that time, he'll be shackled at the ankles by seduction, begging for more of her in the cheap motel bed. She'll stand him up, slip the noose of lust around his fragile neck. He'll grovel; she'll kiss each of his many lashings. Then, she'll pat his head and leave him in the room, hanging. He'll wriggle in what seems like confusion, but she will not cut the cord. After she shuts the door behind her for the last time, she'll spit him over the banister and wipe her mouth with the back of her sleeve.

One of these times, she twists her ankle in a spiked heel as she arrives at her old Chevy Impala. She hobbles into the driver's seat. Yanking down on the visor, she scowls, taking a cold hard look at her tired, dark eyes. Thick black eyeliner and clumpy mascara have bled into bags. A moment of calm comes over her when, unfazed by an older face she doesn't quite recognize, she sees herself in reflection, dried makeup caked in all the ditches. She's comforted by how little she still feels for herself and that nothing has changed.

She leans in, looks closer. Pulls down on her bottom lids, drops Visine into one, the other. Then, as her eyes clear, she's suddenly struck by something innocent left over, something pure. Eyes of the little girl she was, a halo of snowflakes in her hair, standing beside the tiny Japanese maple her father planted in memory of that fat old house cat, Clementine, as they buried her at the base of the tree while her father told her what happens when you die. Don't forget to pray, Faith, he'd said, as she held the wooden box wrapped in a pink bow above the hole at the base of the maple. Pray for what, Daddy? She wiped tears on the back of her sleeve, waiting for his answer before lowering Clementine into the earth. For forgiveness, Faith. Remember? Always pray to be forgiven, he'd said. Clouds gathered as the child stood there wondering what she'd done to kill the cat while her father held her tiny hand. She remembers catching his eyes coming down on her, and they were wild, like a rabbit in a trap.

She'd seen his eyes like that before. Sunday dinner. Her mother forced the family to sit together. Her father at the head of the table, steak knife against glass. Mother watching Father while Faith spooned peas around the plate. Brother would say, This tastes really good, Mother. Doesn't it? Father would grunt and eat. Then, Faith would feel the room suction with silence, heavy and thick, like right before a thunderstorm. Brother would rush her out and stuff her into her small pink bedroom. He'd lock the door. Sometimes, he'd cover her ears. One time, when Faith slithered away from him, she heard Mother screeching like a demon, squealing and crying about how Daddy would go straight to hell for the stealing, the lying, the beatings. But *she* had never actually seen her daddy hurt anyone or break anything. Not with her own two eyes. He'd never stolen from her or said mean things. She asked Brother what he thought, if Daddy was going to hell. Brother said, Father is a bad man, Faith. Seemed to her, no matter what, Brother always took their mother's side.

Faith, on the other hand, was Daddy's little girl. He told her so, and she believed him. They were a team, and they looked out for one another. Like that one summer evening when he took her to the State Fair. Riding his shoulders as always, her shoe came untied and dropped to the grass. He put her down on the State Fair lawn where he had taken her to see Popeye, the star of a famous freak show, skilled at popping his eyes out of their sockets. Then, he set her on Popeye's lap. The man reeked of booze and wore a crumpled plaid suit, while his eyeballs dangled in Faith's face. She'd screamed. Just like that, Daddy swooped her up and saved her.

In the calm after the kitchen storms, Father came only for Faith. Sad and sullen, he'd knock on her bedroom door. She'd let him in and hug him tight. His broad shoulders hunched when she held him in her tiny frame. Then, he'd take her little hands in his as they'd kneel together against the soft edge of her twin bed in front of the open Bible. He'd turn her small body to face him, then lean in to touch his wide forehead to hers, so close she'd smell the musk off his neck. Sometimes his knuckles were swollen, and she'd wait until his eyes were closed to kiss his many scratches. She'd peek to see him bow his head. Then, she'd follow, closing her own eyes down.

Faith, if you want to be forgiven, first you must forgive.

Yes, Daddy.

I'm sorry, my favorite Faithful girl.

For what, Daddy?

I've committed much wrongdoing.

What's wrongdoing?

The things you do that must stay hidden.

I will always forgive you, Daddy. You are forgiven. She felt like a fairy with a wand. Her pardons for him as savior—a fair deal, she thought, like trading Oreos for Mrs. Fields.

Then, soon after Clementine died, late one night, Brother grabbed the girl by her arms and said, Go to your room, Faith. Brother's eyes darted like pinballs. Don't come out until I tell you.

Faith hid under her bed with hands over her ears. She came out just in time to see their neighbor—the one who brought them apple pie last Christmas—close her blinds and turn down the lights while the police hauled her daddy off, hands shackled behind his back. Faith never spoke to that woman again. Wouldn't even look at her.

Later, she begged Brother to tell her what he'd seen. She wanted the truth. He said he'd seen it all, peeking through a crack behind his bedroom door. How her father's gun had aimed slightly upward, angled gently against her mother's right cheek. How at first he swung the thing lawless, above his head, way up in the air, like a cowboy. How her mother's knees buckled when she fell to the ground, her body landing in the shape of devotion as if by memory, hands clasped at her heart, face to the sky. Brother said Jesus must've been watching when Mother fell, begging God to save her. Faith knew right then that God chose to sacrifice one of them for the other. That's why Mother survived.

You're a liar, the girl said. Go get my daddy back.

Brother ignored her. Mother went on to grieve in private, behind closed doors. Faith would hear her crying late at night, alone. She refused to talk to the little girl, to anyone at all, about her sorrow. The home's soundtrack of sobs haunted the girl. That's when Faith decided to take things into her own small hands. She practiced praying, kneeling against the soft edge of her bed. Just like she'd done it with Daddy, she prayed to Jesus to bring him back home to her. Each morning, she'd tumble to her knees before her feet hit the ground, she'd clench her hands together, she'd bend her head down, glaring at the dusty old Bible. Just like she'd seen Daddy do. Young as she was, her first prayer was that he would come back to her. Then, she'd pray to be forgiven for hating her mother—for her weakness and for letting her father get taken away.

When the prayers didn't work and Daddy stayed gone, Faith tried doing research. She found other troubled kids in her class to ask how they did it, the prayer thing. Kids like Edward Mend, always in detention for pulling his pants down and touching himself in front of a girl he liked while hiding behind one of the library shelves during study hour. She assumed he'd know his prayer stuff more than the nicer Sikh boy, Aarav, with his slight smiles and lowered eyes; or the Jewish girl, Tamar, whose father picked her up every day from school exactly as the bell rang with the same bear hug and hand-holding; definitely more than Banko, the Buddhist boy, who hardly spoke and ate a special lunch obviously packed for him by loving parents. No, Faith needed a God that could produce results, really make things happen. It would take a lot to break her daddy out. Plus, good kids like them wouldn't know any prayers about forgiveness. In the end, she went with Ed Mend. He gave her pointers during lunch hour, like what position to hold her hands, how to kneel and bow, what, in God's name, to say. Then he pulled his pants down. His naked body excited her. Later, she asked Jesus for forgiveness as she'd been taught. She reported all her wrongdoings, even her naughty thoughts about Ed Mend, and went back to her old routine.

Until she turned thirteen. The Boy she first loved was like Jesus himself. She stopped praying at night only to close her eyes and fondle herself thinking of him. In her small twin bed, she'd imagine the Boy wearing Bermudas and walking along a beach, sculpted muscles, tanned skin. The Boy's windblown locks curled, flowing to his shoulders. He'd remove his sunglasses, tip them toward her, and wink, then smile, as if she was the only girl in the whole world. Back then, she didn't even know which was the right spot to touch between her peach-fuzzed legs.

Suddenly then, at the wheel of the Impala, Faith thinks of her mother. Years have passed since they've seen each other. When Faith was young, after her father had been taken, she'd watch her mother from across the dinner table in dim light. The map of crevices along her cheekbone, up her jaw. She'd come to memorize the terrain of that face—how shadows lodged in the furrow of a deep wedge down the woman's right cheek, how darkness pooled in the puckers of a starfish scar near her temple. Sometimes, she'd want to touch her, but then anger would stop her. She'd remember how Mother refused to allow her to visit Father. How taking his collect calls from prison was forbidden. How lonely her daddy must be without his little girl having ever gone to see him.

Father's been locked up so long, Faith doubts he'd even recognize her. Assault with a deadly weapon. Guilty. Intent to kill. Guilty. Plus, a prior for slapping an old ex-girlfriend. But he was a kid back then. And they'd fallen short of proving anything, really. He stopped calling after a while. Her mother's doing. She'd tried to go see him a few times. Not taking visitors, the guard said. She knows he doesn't want his little girl to see him that way, all caged up, like some animal. Oddly, she often wonders if he remembers planting Clementine's tree. She imagines him staring out the slivered window of his cell thinking about how tall the tree is now. Or if she made it through the winters to live at all.

In her car, Faith turns her mouth up at the corners, pinches her cheeks. She draws new lines in black under her eyes like a cat, dabs her face with powder. Grabs a smoke from her purse, practices drawing in and blowing out as if on camera. Pull your shit together, Faith, she says in her most imposing wicked voice. No Misters she knows want a good girl underneath, not really. They'll say they do. But she knows that the sinful parts are what will keep them even remotely interested.

Turning the key, she swats at the cross hanging from her mirror to check behind her. A plastic ruby that's come unglued drops from the hand of the little Jesus straight into a can of week-old Diet Mountain Dew crusted to the console. She takes this as a sign that things are still right on track to falling apart. She backs out of the motel parking lot pounding her fists to *Sweet Child O' Mine* off the radio like a reflex, with the fleeting feeling of being a teenager again.

There will be many mostly-married Misters throughout her forties. Faith's practice of catch and release becomes a meditative state of existence, like fly fishing. Then, one catch snags her line completely. This one is handsome. Not sexy like her usual unshaven, punishing type. No, this Mister is landscaped like a perfect French formal garden. He's manicured; he smells good; he wears a matching striped tie. He smiles gently when he speaks to her. This Mister is divorced, available.

Early on, the Mister insists on talking to her about his three young children after passion gets the best of him. Naked, he lays his head on her breast, eyes pointed down the length of her bare torso, one leg folded across her abdomen. He reminds her of a fetus. She wants to hate him when she feels one tear run off his nose and roll down the slope of her ribcage. She touches the top of his head as if soothing a child. Her touch seems to open a valve in him. Tears overflow the cask of her navel and pool on her torso until her bare stomach is an ice rink thawed by his pain. Determined to feel less for this Mister, she stares beyond him, out the window at the neon motel sign flashing VACANCY. She imagines her own father in a cage. She reminds herself how fathers who think they're good, even the godly ones, rarely are. How even the best fathers, even the pious ones, who pick you up at the waist, toss you into the air, throw you over broad quarterback shoulders, sing songs to you that will carve into the memory like scars, will eventually put you down. *Even ones like you*, she thinks while petting his sweaty hair.

His daughter, she'll outgrow the shoulder rides. He may say something like, *You're just too heavy*, or, *You're a big girl now, I can't carry you like that anymore*, or he may say nothing at all. But somehow he'll tell her. After years of showing her off, he'll decide she's not his little girl anymore. She won't know this yet, while she grins wide, all gums, feeling like his shiny crown as she grabs onto tufts of his thick black curls sprouting through her fingers. She'll pull up on his hair like the reins of her very own black stallion, like the one they'll see together in the theater, front row; one of his hands, one of hers, down the mouth of an extra-large imitation butter bucket. He'll try to hide his tears, but she'll see him cry. And she'll make sure to tuck away her smile in the dark theater when his face is pointed at the screen. Faith comes back to the moment with the Mister, kisses him with an open mouth, all tongue, just to shut him up.

He dresses, his striped tie loose around his neck. She's naked, wrapped in the white bedsheet. The Mister stands before her. He wraps himself around her as if the sex, the tears, mean she will be his lover forever. He kisses her forehead, and when she pulls her face away, she notices his eyelashes are still wet. His hands graze the length of her backbone, and somehow, she feels some kind of virtue in the touch of his warm fingertips. His candor makes her shiver. Suddenly, she doesn't want to let him go.

She continues to see the handsome Mister longer than any of the others. Weekly. Same motel. Same room. #10. Her choice. When he asks her to have a meal outdoors, a picnic in public, she says, Let's just keep it simple, silly. I will meet you in #10. I'm going to blow your mind this time.

She comes to learn his children's names through the time he spends lingering around in #10. What sports they play, when their birthdays are, how his voice changes when he talks about them. After sex, when the smell of his underarm makes her wet all over again, she draws blood biting down on her tongue. As he squeezes her thigh, she claws at her cuticles, yearning for him with the swell and shift of the vein running up his forearm. When he makes her laugh, she sucks in her gut and swallows hard. She's desperate to enjoy him less.

Just let me in, Faith.

You're not allowed, Mister.

I'm not going anywhere, he says.

Slowly, over time, her body gives over. She begins looking forward—to how clean he is for her, how he likes to make her come first, how he wraps his arms around her when they're done, how he wants to stay with her even after the sex is over. Each time they're together, he cries, for one reason or another, and she begins to like this, too. She looks forward to his tears.

I am so happy when we're together, Faith …

I feel everything when I'm with you …

I just don't know which box to put you in …

I need to make a box for you …

I love my kids, Faith …

I really, really do …

I think I might love …

Stop, Faith says.

I think I might love you, he says.

Just stop.

Faith knows time can turn any place at all into home. Even a cell. Even a motel room with this man. Even a man with three kids he'll never want her to meet. She begins to feel at home with these people who don't belong to her.

One day, Faith has time to kill before meeting her Mister. She runs into an old friend from high school at her usual spot, Tucci's, a bar where the popular clique spent lunch hours all the way through senior year of high school. Faith never made the cut. Although she hasn't seen the woman in years, she remembers her mostly because of the time she got drunk and puked red wine at Tonya's house, all over her parents' white bear-skin rug, shaming herself in front of the Boy, her biggest crush of that year.

I never see you here. You still live in town? Faith asks.

I got out a few years ago. Finally. Headed to Chicago. I'm back for a while, though, taking care of my mother. Cancer. The doctors aren't giving her longer than six months. Tonya whispers this prognosis.

I'm sorry to hear that. Faith is not sorry, not really. What are you doing to cope? she asks, out of politeness.

I pray, Tonya says. A lot.

You? *Pray?* Faith laughs. The one who let all the guys from the team into your pants one-by-one?

My pants? You're the one who had gum in your hair for days from making out with Davis Scott in the bushes. I think you let him finger you at Fox Hall Theater that same night. Or was that Drew Martin? Could never keep them all straight.

God, remember all those guys from the team? Like Nate Thomas. We got high with him on the basketball courts of Lakeshore Elementary. And remember that one time? When I drank all that wine? I think we were in like eighth grade, Faith says, thinking about the Boy.

Oh right, the rug night, how could I forget? First of many messy ones, Tonya laughs and rolls her eyes. She takes another sip off the top of her martini. Faith finishes her own and waves her hand at the waitress for another. They reflect on their childhoods like looking in a rearview mirror.

You remember that one Boy, right? I wonder whatever happened to him. I think about him every so often, Faith says.

Oh *that* Boy ... right. Your first, Tonya says. That Boy turned out to be bad news. I heard he's doing time in Green Bay Correctional. People say he raped a girl in college. Guess you dodged a bullet on that one.

Maybe, Faith says.

You okay? You're white as a ghost.

Does it work? The prayer thing, I mean, Faith manages.

It helps. Me more than her, I think. How's your mother? All that shit that went down.

She's fine. Just fine.

Did her face heal? I mean, God, he actually tried to shoot her. You're a bigger woman than me if you don't fucking hate him. I know he's your father, but ... such a shame.

Faith sets her drink down and skids her moist hands along the face of the table, gathering them toward her. Under the table, she clasps her hands into a net, squeezing them together tightly between her bare thighs. She holds her breath until she's drowning. Then she makes a run for the door.

It's late by the time she arrives at room #10. He's already naked and lying on the bed when she walks through the door. She kisses him hard, forcibly. He smiles, looks into her eyes, touches along her forehead. She kisses him again, this time harder. He pushes her back from him and laughs as if she's role playing. This makes him hard, her exerting such force over him. He tries to cradle her underneath him, to slide his hand behind the small of her back and draw her hips close. She slithers out from underneath him and mounts him as if riding a bull Her hair is wild; she's completely untamed, throwing her head back and forth.

He doesn't seem to see her cry. Like magic, he slips out of roughness when they're finished, lovingly spooning her, running his hand along her thigh, her arm, her ear. He softens like warm water. Faith stays wrapped in the sheet, curled around the pillow, while he's in the bathroom cleaning up.

She stands slowly. At the window, she lights a cigarette. Only one car slowly makes its way down the road this late at night. A man is driving, his woman in the passenger seat. When they pass, VACANCY flashes, and Faith sees the two together, laughing. Blue neon turns them ghostly like two dancing skeletons. She draws the curtains, sits heavy on the bed, the sheet still clamped at her chest.

She looks around the confined room—a television on its stand, a crooked old dresser, a toilet reflected in the closet mirror. Her father's cell would be much smaller than this. On the nightstand, a Bible. She doesn't remember seeing it there before. She checks the door. Chain still hangs on its lock. She drops her cigarette into a plastic cup of water. Then, she touches the book with one timid hand like a child to a hot stove. On its cover, she traces the word *Holy* with her finger. The book is heavy in her hand. She drops the sheet from around her to cup both hands under the spine. As the pages fall open, an edge, like a feather, brushes along the underside of her bare breast. Her shoulders round while she leans into the lines as if in worship, hair coming forward around her face.

Against the sound of the shower running, she reads aloud, each word in her own voice. *Bearing with one another and* … the Boy. He bore down on her while she bled, stealing her very first time at thirteen. When she snuck out late one school night wearing tight jeans and a shirt buttoned down to her bra to meet him at the elementary school playground. She remembers seeing a spiderweb tangled in a small cross hanging above her mother's door frame while she stalled with guilt at the threshold. She remembers thinking it was weakness that made her mother whimper like that in the middle of the night. She prayed. Only to not get caught.

… *if one has a complaint against another* … Snot was frozen into crust around the edges of each of her nostrils, wet hairspray had glued stringy pieces to the sides of her face. When her teeth knocked against his, their tongues fumbling around, stabbing at the other's, she thought only of her father. And when the Boy shoved one frozen hand down her pants and the other up her bra, rubbing and pinching, she thought only of needing forgiveness. Virgin snow had traveled up her pants legs to her crotch from the walk through the hushed neighborhood to meet him. She was almost frozen when he forced himself inside her, so it hurt more like being crushed than ruptured.

… *forgiving each other* … After, she was rigid and stiffened, with chattering teeth like a marionette. He wrapped her into his jacket, held her against his chest. His hair smelled like coconuts and sweat. He reached toward her face to tuck the hair behind her ear. His eyes were round like Magic 8-Balls with flecks of gold, lashes thick and curly. A snowflake landed at the tip of one, bounced onto his nose when he blinked then kissed her.

… *as the Lord has forgiven you* … When she buried her drops of blood with her boots, the snow made the sound of Styrofoam rubbing against itself. The Boy said, Okay, well, we should do this again sometime. I'll call you. She asked him to. Call her again. On the walk home, she cried with fear. She had the mature sense, like a dawning, that later in life it would take much more terrifying things to traumatize her.

... so you must also forgive.

She'd asked for it.

Hadn't she?

A sharp breath drawn in from her nose floods her lungs. Faith looks up from the holy book. She clings to that breath as if at the edge of a high dive. Her lips purse. She falls to her knees at the edge of the bed, her pew. She slams the book shut, squeezing it between her palms, praying for redemption, until her fingernails go white.

She feels him there, the Mister, standing above her, cool against her heat. When he rests a hand on her bare back, drops from his wet hair land on her nape. She straightens slightly as the water slides down the round of her spine between her shoulders to the small of her back. He moves her enough to inch in on the edge of the bed before her. Then, he lifts her naked torso and drapes her along the length of his lap. She reaches her arms around the folds of his waist, tucks her head into the crease of his hip as if curling into a womb.

What happened to you, Faith? You can tell me.

Are you a religious man, Abel?

I believe we are all forgiven in the end.

How can you be so sure?

Belief itself is enough to get me by, says Abel.

She stands then. They dress each other. Facing her, he wraps her blouse around her shoulders, buttons it from the top, down. She slips his tie around his neck, tightens it loosely. She takes his hand in one of hers, the Bible in the other. When they are outside, she says, We will never come to this room together again. Say goodbye to #10.

At the car, he opens the passenger door for her. He revs the engine and turns up the heat. Snow has just begun to fall. Her hand is on the Bible as Abel hears about the Boy. Snowfall gathers thick on the windshield, bluer in the break of day. When she says, I think I asked for it. Am I broken? Abel says, Your cracks are lined with gold. When she says, Bulletproof glass won't protect me from those Magic 8-Ball eyes, Abel says, All you have to do is look at mine. Carefully then, they drive away. There will be ice on the road to Green Bay Correctional. They'll have to take their time.

VIDA

TO TELL YOU about Vida, I have to go back to when I'm fifteen, and all I want is a good fight. To when I don't know nothing—*nada*—about how love works. When el amor solamente means bad things are coming. I love Mami. Then she dies with a needle in her arm. Y Papi? He's shot dead on the streets of East LA before I'm out of diapers. I don't remember him, but I guess I got a little bit of his love left over on me, after all. A brand that never goes away. See, before he died, Mami let him name me. He said I'd turn out just like the coyote, just like him. Wild. They say Papi was a smart man on the streets. Not smart enough to stay alive, I say. He was smart about naming me, though. Name's Wiley. Es verdad, suits me just fine.

When Mami dies after Papi dies, I get shoved off to Abuela for a few years. I still got my Abuela's ring, the thing she gave me at her bedside days before she died. To remember her by, she said. I wear the ring on my left hand on the finger that means you're attached. Or committed. I can't remember which.

Abuela doesn't want me at first, I can tell. Hardly says much between her missing front teeth. But then she starts to cook for me. Pozole and pastor. Chiles roasted right on the burner of the gas stove. Comida in big pots and pans like she's feeding an army, but it's only us two. And tortillas. Not those kind you get at El Mercadito in the package. The real ones. And not in some tortilla press, neither. No, she mashes the masa by hand.

Until the cancer.

At the end, she only eats plain chicken, no skin. Any smells in our apartment make her sicker. One time, I try to make her favorite—café con leche. I even run a cinnamon stick along her cheese grater for more flavor on the top. Then I carry it to her, wobbling on a tray. She pukes in the trash bin next to her bed. After that, no more cooking. No more smells of chiles and chocolate. All aromas are banned. Her body turns into a tiny peanut in its shell with all that loose wrinkled skin.

I'm the one who finds her one day, head slumped. Dead in a straight-backed chair. She made it all the way from her bed to the TV room to die. I remember wondering which telenovela was worth all that extra energy just to up and die for. I do not cry. I just wonder.

When Abuela dies, I get put in the system. I'm on my way to Vida. Strange details stick out when love's coming your way but she's not here yet. Things that, after someone's come and gone, you'll want to savor—sweet and sour—like tamarindo on your tongue. Really, you don't get to choose how things look in your head. Memories are like my street art—once it's tagged, the colors stand, good *and* bad, splattered across the mind like a crime. Mi Vida? She's all the colors in one. My mural.

The house had cracked paint. Yellow—mustard, more like, with the way the sun beats down. Sucks all the shine out. East LA sun makes for angry summers. You can see the heat come off the street, black tar gone soft like oil in a fryer. Everyone's a badass in August, and everyone wants a fight. People get all riled up when it's that hot. Me? Not yet. I just wanted to get the shit over with. The introductions and whatnot. I know how it goes, a new foster home. I been in the system long enough to have the lowdown on how fitting in with families takes time. You got to remember the small things that make up a family's memory. You got to let them see you cry—at least once, I've learned—to get them to like you. I never stay long enough. For me, crying doesn't come easy.

So, I'm on the porch smoking. The foster parents seem to know they can't stop us from smoking. Most teens in the system smoke. Passes the time waiting for the next move. There's always another move. I do a French inhale. Some kid from a home way back taught me that. I got my hat pulled down low on my forehead. Flat-billed LA Dodgers like Papi wore, they say.

This time, my caseworker has taken me herself. Said it was no trouble, she had the time. I stand on the porch watching her from behind. She's searching for her briefcase in the car. *Stay here, Wiley. Don't move. Damn kids. Always causing trouble.* She's got her whole body shoved into the back seat moving things around. Her skirt rides up, and I can see the top part of her pantyhose where the girdle starts. She's a big woman—Ms. B. That's what the kids call her. Says, This way, it's easier to remember, Wiley. Just one letter. She reminds me of my Abuela—her size.

I put my smoke out before Ms. B gets back from her car. *Put that cigarette out! Make things easy on yourself for once, Wiley. No one wants a kid who smokes.* Ms. B and me stand at the door with her briefcase. Her size seems to make her sweat more than most. Also, she seems nervous. I know she wants me placed without trouble this time. It's gotta be at least ninety-five degrees, and that kind of heat don't help things. Her hands slip. She drops her pen at my feet. Says she wants me to really feel safe and at home with these nice folks. She tugs at the elastic waist on her skirt. Says to act right and everything will be fine, she says. She says, This time might be different, Wiley. Be a good girl. You're almost an adult now. Act your age. I stop listening after the nice folks part. Plus, remember, I'm only fifteen.

I think to myself, Just say it, woman. Say what you want to say: Do not lie; do not steal; do not shout, FUCK YOU, LADY at the foster mother; do not scream, GO SUCK A COCK at the foster father; do not rage or hit other kids. *You East LA kids are no joke, Wiley. I know you're angry.* Do not tag the bedroom walls with Sharpie; do not tag the outside gate with spray paint; do not run away; do not stay; do not waste my motherfucking time. I know what she wants to say: Do not be your real damaged self. What she means is, *Hide.* Instead, she sweats. And lies.

There's grass there. Greener than at most homes. I think there are tomatoes growing. They have hot peppers in old, plastic paint buckets. Red and yellow and orange. My Abuela ate Hungarian hots raw, right off the stem. Said they were hotter than any habanero. She'd sweat and snort. Wipe her forehead with her sleeve then use the cuff to blow her nose. The water would run and run and run from her forehead like a busted faucet. Never complained, just took the heat. Never bitched about the cancer, neither. No one might have guessed she was dying except that she couldn't wear the wig in summer. Too hot. She was tough. I think she loved me. Until she died. Then she was just ... dead. Not so tough, after all.

I act nice to Ms. B. I try to show the caseworkers respect. *Show me some respect, goddamnit. No wonder they don't want you.* I don't know why. No point, really. She got so many kids, soon she won't remember my name. They might give me someone new next time. I don't want someone new. Ms. B's okay. *Tuck your shirt in, Wiley. And pull your pants up. You've got to look more presentable. I want them to like you. You know how many cases I got right now? Too many. I need this one to stick.* I bend down to grab her pen. Holding the thing out for her, I notice the porch is clean, swept. Next plot over is an empty lot where another house should have been, but no house, just brown grass and trash. There's a rusted-out metal barrel with a grate on top off to the corner of the lot. On its side, someone tagged *QUE TENGAS UN BUEN DÍA* with a little devil to the side. I wonder what it might be like to choose how a day feels. The devil makes me smile. The front yard here is completely fenced in.

I stay quiet, of course. I am no idiota. In a way, I want them to like me too this time. See, I'm feeling tired of being shuffled around like a domino. Also, Ms. B and me, we have a relationship now like she's my mama, but her only duty is to make sure we go our separate ways. Somehow, I want to do right by her. *Take that hat off, Wiley. You look like a little boy. The fosters want to know what kind of girl they're getting.* I'm gonna do Ms. B a solid, so I take my hat off. I never take this hat off. I tuck it under my armpit. Ms. B rolls her eyes, snatches her pen from my hand. Then, she faces the door. Pen. Click. Click. I look at my feet, hands down my pockets. She rings the bell, again. We stand on a mat that says, *Home Sweet Home* in curly letters. The *Sweet* part is larger than the letters spelling *Home*. I let my backpack slide from my shoulder to the ground. We wait.

Ms. B's back always gets straighter when the foster parents open the door. *Stand up, girl. They're coming.* This one is a tall man with a big gut. He's dressed nice enough—button shirt, decent pants. He wears a leather belt. A wide metal buckle is front and center with an

American flag painted into the steel grooves like a banner. He rubs his fingers along the front of the buckle, then tucks his thumbs into his pockets. One of his buttons is undone where the shirt is tucked into his waist.

This the new one?

Yes, sir, Ms. B says.

Wiley, right?

That's right, she says.

Nice to meet you, I say, eyes down. *You need to learn some manners, Wiley.*

Well, let's get on with it, then, he says.

He moves aside, opens the door wide, propped by his foot. Ms. B touches my back with her sweaty palm to nudge me in. I lean back into her for a moment. When I bend forward to pick up my backpack, my hat falls to the ground. I grab it fast. Something about the father makes me not want to wear it. Instead, I bend the bill and stuff the hat down the side of my backpack. I slide both arms into the straps and tighten. Then, I tuck my hair behind my ears. I have to try hard to straighten up.

When I'm inside, he locks the deadbolt behind us. I turn to look for Ms. B. Through the small glass window of the front door, I see her again from behind. She's untucking her blouse from her skirt. She walks faster, stalls at the gate, already fumbling for her car keys in her purse. I hear the beep when she unlocks her car and closes the gate behind her. Then, she glances one last time toward the house. She shakes her head, checks the gate again. To make sure it shut. Sometimes I wonder who waits for her at her own home. Through the small pane of glass, I know she can't see me anymore.

♕

The thing about new homes—you can tell a lot of what you need to know in the first five minutes. I can tell right away there's no mother here. But I don't ask questions about that. *Don't ask so many questions next time. No one wants a nosy child.* The shades are drawn across the windows of the front room. There's one brown couch, two wooden chairs, a big screen TV on a black stand. On the coffee table, a cigar sits in an ashtray on top of a couple men's magazines. The *TIME* magazine has Donald Trump on the cover. The whole place smells like burnt popcorn and Budweiser. I look at the walls. The only thing hanging is one framed photo. In the middle, it's the foster father, younger, with his arms around two other men in uniform. One has a big gun strapped across his chest. In the background, there's only desert sand. Above the photo, a wooden cross. There's no green anywhere in this place. No fake plants in the room, no real ones either. No flowers, no doilies or coasters, no paintings, no clutter. No color to anything at all. The man's in charge.

This is my room, got it? he says.

Yes, sir. *ESTÚPIDO.*

You ain't allowed to laze around in here, got it?

Yes, sir. *CHINGA TU MADRE.*

And in this house, there ain't no woman to clean up after you, got it?

Yes, sir. *HIJO DE PUTA.*

So, you're gonna have to clean up your own mess, got it?

Yes, sir. *Each family has their own rules, Wiley. You're going to have to learn to fit in and adapt to differences.* How many kids live here? I ask.

With you, makes three. I'm on the light side with fosters right now.

I stretch my neck to look past him down the hallway toward

the back of the house. There's a kitchen back there. A couple other rooms, too. Doors are shut. I can't get a feel except that I'm not allowed back there.

My room's upstairs then? I ask.

Kids' rooms are all upstairs.

I follow him up with my backpack held tight. He still has his work boots on. On the lower stair beneath him, I see mud caked in the treads of the boots. A small, sheathed, fixed blade hangs on his belt. He's a lumberjack of a man—gruff, this one. Still resembles the soldier in his photo but rougher and wider with more chinks in his skin.

He takes me through the hallway with his thumbs hooked on his belt like he's a guard checking on the inmates. On that side, I got Santos. Santos Ramirez. He hasn't been here long, he says, tapping the door with his knuckle. He points ahead. You're at the end of the hall. You share with Vida.

She another foster? I ask.

Sure is, he says. He gets quiet, sort of sucks himself in. Then I hear him whisper her name, Vida Arenas Lopez, and way under his breath, Sweet little thing. I notice the color change in his face— red to pale—when I look at him after he says it. He's tense, tight in the mouth, like a kid caught cussing in church.

Vida, I say. Then, *Vida, Vida, Vida* ... and I don't know why I sing out like that, but I do, I say her name over and over, I do. I haven't even met her yet, but I want him to know our names don't belong to him. Since then, I've learned that unfit love can make you do unreasonable things even before you put a face to it.

Finally, he cuts in, snaps, Get yourself situated. We eat at 6:00 p.m., sharp. You miss dinner, fend for yourself. That's how it works around here, got it?

Yes, sir, I say. When his back's turned, I give him a one-finger salute.

In my room, I toss my bag on the top bunk. New kids always take the top. I take a breath. It's like the first gasp a newborn takes in the world after the womb. And you're all alone for that one moment. Until you're not. I know there's a girl in the room behind me because I smell her. I see colors when I smell her. Pinks and reds splattered wild on some white wall like spray paint from the can. I already know her name: *Vida, Vida, Vida.*

You can have the bottom, she says behind me.

I can take the top, I say. No problem.

I'm used to sleeping up there.

Whatever you say.

I feel safe sleeping closer to the stars, she says.

I turn toward her and cross my arms. You been in this home long? I ask.

A few months.

How is it here?

She shrugs, turns away from me. De miedo, pero, it's okay, she says. I wonder what she's afraid of. Kids like us learn how to box and bury fear like a body.

What's your name?

Vida, she says, hushed.

She reaches her hand toward me like a shake, but somehow I come from underneath with my arm, so her hand lands in mine like a ball to a glove, palms cradled, face up. I don't mean to touch her like that. I don't mean to like it when I do. But I do.

I'm Wiley, I say and close my hand around hers just a bit.

Silly name for a chola, she says. How'd you get a name like that? The coyote.

You wild?

Maybe I am.

Should I be scared of you, little Wiley? she laughs.

Cuidada, I say. Careful. *If you keep acting like a wild animal, Wiley, no family will take you.*

Pues, you might be tough, she says, but I think it's pretty, your name. The way she says my name, how her tongue rolls around— W-I-L-E-Y—the word seems safe in her mouth. Like somehow, she's caught me, too.

When I meet her, Vida's seventeen, almost old enough to get out. You can tell by how she tiptoes around the yellow house, bending herself around things, like she's trying to disappear ahead of time. Como un fantasma, like a ghost. Some would say I was too young to fall for her. Tal vez, maybe, pero yo sabía. I know how I feel. Lo siento todo. I feel *everything* after so long of feeling nothing at all.

I'm in the yellow house for weeks, and still, I can't sleep. I hate the pinche place. Especially at night. I hate being upstairs with no AC in summer heat, and there's a burning smell in my nose, but no fire. Summer cicadas buzz on haywire, and I can hear the fiesta of roaches in cracks of the walls like tiny tap dancers. I got a can of spray paint in my backpack. Always do. I imagine lighting the whole room on fire with my art. Light it up with flames and demons and every vulgar word I know.

I'm on my bottom bunk. She's on top. I got my arm crooked behind my head, elbow in the air, watching the coils of her mattress worm when she moves her body. I know Vida's awake, tambien. When she can't sleep, she sings. At first, I hate her for it. I hate how she can stay so calm lying there in the dark. For me, the sleeplessness makes me angry, like having my hands tied behind my back in a fight. I want to scream, break free. But not Vida. She just sings and waits.

One night, I'm listening. I know she's still awake, but barely, because she's humming, no words. What's that song? I ask. She tells me it's *Oh! Susanna*, and then she keeps singing, so soft, like some kind of lullaby, and I recognize the tune—not the words, no—the sound, somehow deep, way down, in my bones. I feel her voice in my toes. I don't remember falling asleep, but I do. The girl can sing.

I don't know if it's the song that makes me dream or Vida's voice. That night, I see them all there. All the ghosts. Mami with the needle hanging out her arm. Abuela—bald—wig in her hand. Even my Papi's there, I think that's him. He's got the Dodgers hat tucked under his armpit, and the gun that killed him in his hand. Then, it's him there, the foster father, el señor, he's got his belt in his hand. He buckles the metal American flag around Vida's waist and tightens, and he's yanking her toward him like she's leashed. When he shuts the door, he puts his finger to his lips, Shhhh, he whispers, shush. I wake. They're gone. The ghosts. I'm sweating. I jump. Bang my head on the top bunk. It's already morning.

You okay, wild Wiley? Vida leans down from her bed above.

Bien, bien. I'm fine, I say.

You were crying in your sleep.

Fuck that. Was not.

Okay, okay, Vida laughs. Guess what?

¿Qué?

Today's my birthday.

No mames wey.

Sí. I'm eighteen.

Holy shit.

I'm going to get out of here.

When?

As soon as I can, she says and lifts her mattress. I almost have enough.

I don't know where she got that money. No importa. All that matters to me is how she *trusts* me. I don't know why she trusts me. And that don't matter neither. I feel valuable, like when Abuela let me use her kitchen knife for the first time—bonded by the risk we share. Like finally I have someone who wants my loyalty. That's the thing with young love. More heart, less investigation.

It's a Saturday. Vida's eighteenth. I remember because the foster father's gone, and we don't have school. Santos is still in his room when Vida and me tiptoe downstairs. She wants una fiesta, she says, in the empty house. For her birthday. In foster care, privacy is like pinning the tail on the donkey. You only win it when you're not looking.

I'm standing aside from her, watching. I got my arms crossed at my chest, one leg hooked over the other, leaning against the door-frame. My hat's pulled low. She's rummaging through the kitchen searching for booze, flinging cabinet doors open, one after the other, yanking on drawers, and I'm just standing there wondering what's this puta gonna find in some junk drawer that can fuck us up? I smile. She's rushing for no good reason. We know he'll be gone for the day. His agenda's penciled in on a calendar. Says right there, he'll be busy until 5:00. El señor is strict about time, having been in the military, so I think we're in the clear.

Finally, she finds a bottle under the sink, in the back with the cleaners. Cazadores. Cheap tequila, but at least it's something.

Then, she finds a couple limes rolling around the back of the crisper drawer in the fridge. Grabs a knife from the drawer. Cuts around the brown parts to make slices. She grabs the salt and says, Tú y yo. You and me, Wiley. On the porch. Ahoríta.

I look at her then. Holding the bottle in one hand, limes in the palm of her other, juice running down her arm. Suddenly, I think of Mami before all the drugs, before the leaving and the dying, before all this. I mean I actually feel her rhythm in the room, way down in my gut. I see her in Vida's shine—so pretty like Mami used to be. Mami loved to dance. She'd play the radio and when Santana came on with *Oye Como Va*, she'd move and sing, she'd spread her body around the room, moving her hips, sucking on limes against her lips after shots from a tiny glass. Mami y yo, I'm so little, happy, she dances with me, *Baila conmigo mi chiquitita, te amo mucho, muchísimo*, she says and takes my tiny fingers in her hand held high so I can twirl under her arm and spin. She catches me and won't let me go. And I can't believe it, how much of Mami I feel when I see Vida.

What do you say, wild Wiley? Vida says, holding the bottle out.

My shoulders roll down my back from up near my ears. My chest opens. She's so bright, brighter than the graffiti in my mind. She's blood-red jewels and pink roses, orange shades of fire and flames, yes, she is, she is. She's the boldest red in her face, at the rounds of each cheek. But there is more. I stall. I stare at her body's surface like right before I tag a wall. She's the white light of a blank canvas *behind* the paint, she has the softness of diamond shine and the warmth of gold. *Pura Vida.*

Claro que sí, I say. It's on.

We're on the porch smoking and taking shots. When Santos comes downstairs, we invite him. It's a celebration, we say. ¡Feliz cumpleaños, Vida! No te preocupes, el señor is gone till 5:00! we say.

We lick the backs of our hands, sprinkle salt for each other. Vida pours. We clink glasses, take the shot, lick the salt, suck the lime, and again. I sit next to Vida on the bench. We're so close, her arm rests along my thigh. It's got to be almost a hundred degrees. Booze helps us forget about the heat.

You guys want to play a game? Santos asks.

Sure, Vida says.

Birthday girl goes first, he says.

I stay quiet watching Santos. He's leaning against the porch railing. I see him eyeing one of the buckets that el señor grows peppers in. A small orange habanero hangs from its stem. I know that the small bright ones are usually the hottest. I look at Vida. She doesn't seem to know what's coming. But I do, I do.

Vida, truth or dare? Santos says.

Dare, she answers, fast.

Santos leans over and plucks the pepper, smiling wide. The pepper's dangling off its stem when he hands it off to Vida. Cómetelo, he says, the whole thing.

That girl, just when I think she might be soft. She doesn't even bat an eye when she snatches the thing from Santos and pops it in her mouth. I watch her the whole time. She keeps her eyes on Santos. Chews twice or three times. Then swallows. She swipes her hands together, opens her empty mouth wide at him, and says, ¿Bueno? ¿Qué más? like what else you got for me, chico?

I stare, can't get my gaze off her. When Vida's eyes start to water from the sting, I see Abuela clear as day, tough as nails, chomping on her Hungarian hots, wiping the sweat from her face. They're bigger than life to me—both of them—and strong—fuerte, fuerte, fuerte—in color, como el fuego, blazing like fire. I don't know if it's the tequila that's got me, but oh—mi corazón—my heart pumps me full of feelings I've never had before. Seeing Vida. Remembering mi familia. I'm bursting.

Santos looks stunned when Vida stays quiet with the heat of el chile in her mouth. Suddenly, she gasps and spits, and we all break out laughing like hyenas, hopping up and down like little conejitos.

Your turn, Wiley, says Santos. Truth or dare?

Dare, I say. Bring it on, puto.

I *dare* you to kiss Vida. En la boca.

My heart stops. I mean it actually stops beating. When it starts up again, I feel the thing bulge in my chest and plummet to my toes.

No way, Santos, I say. Not going to happen. I'm looking down when I say it, and I feel my face red and burnt up like el diablo. I shake my head fast. My hands tingle. Even my ears are hot. My stomach sloshes with tequila like a washing machine.

Está todo bien, wild Wiley, Vida says.

What? Are you serious?

Let's just do it.

I shove my hands down my pockets. I've never kissed anyone, much less una chica bonita, the prettiest girl I've ever seen with hips as round as her lips, big brown eyes, and the kind of hair that's made for a doll, like black silk. Vida gets up from the bench, stands to my front. Then, she reaches out to me, holding out her hands to help me up.

I don't think about doing it. I just do. I kiss her. Un beso. One time. Right then, it starts to drizzle. You see, I remember the rain—I will always remember the rain—because in LA, summer is like the Mojave, and it just never did. Rain. I remember thinking about my mama with the needle in her arm, hoping that she felt like this—the one kiss—right before she died. One kiss. On the jawbone, accidentally, at its angle, just beneath her ear. Our lips only graze one another's. But I want her. My sister. My *pinche* sister. ¿Mi amor? My lifer. I go red. How could I? Mi Vida. Then, just like that, it's over. I pull back some. She's still close when she whispers, Tranquila amor, tranquila. Then she says, Tienes que salir de aquí. Ir a correr. Run far away from him.

¿Qué dijo? I say, and step away from her. What did you say?

Vida releases my hands. That's when I see him standing there under the frame of the front door. Our foster father. I bite my tongue. He must've parked in the alley behind the house, come in through the back door. He's early.

What the fuck is this? he says. You all think you can have a party in MY home?

Santos says, It's Vida's birthday, then backs away. I watch Vida when her body buckles, collapsing into the bench. It seems to me she's trying to fold herself up into a thing too small for him to notice. Suddenly, she's so small, tan pequeña, and somehow I know that he's coming for her. That this is not the first time he's had her.

I take my hat off and set it gently on Vida's lap. I turn toward him. I stand taller than I know I am, feet wide, arms crossed at my chest. Then, I move my body to shield hers, directly between them. I block him from getting to her. Sitting behind me, her knees touch the backs of my calves. The father stomps. One boot. Two boots. Slats bend where wood is rot. He's closer to me. The Cazadores bottle wobbles on the porch when he steps. He grabs the bottle. Hurls it over the fence into the empty lot next door. He hits the rusted-out metal barrel square on the mark where the little devil's tagged. Glass shatters. Vida flinches.

You, he says to Vida, you're coming with me. Get up.

He tries to shove me aside to get to her. I puff my chest. No,

I say. Don't touch her.

Move aside, girl.

You're not taking her.

He pushes his hands down on my shoulders as if he's trying to drown me. Pressing, hard, to sit me down. I lock my knees. I go nowhere. I squeeze myself tighter, arms around my chest.

No, I say, No.

He's yelling now, Move your ass, you freak of a girl. I feel spit on my face, he's so close.

No, I yell. No!

Finally, he gets a good grip on my shoulder. I see that blade he wears hanging off his belt. He shoves me. Hard. I fall to the side. I grab for the knife as I fall. I miss. His belt breaks from my grab. I'm on the ground, his broken belt beside my head. I lie flat, long, so he has to step over me to get to her. He picks up the belt. Finds the knife alongside the bench. When he steps over me, I see between his legs from the ground. Then, he's in front of her. Looking down on her. He threads the belt through each loop, secures the knife, never taking his eyes off her.

Vida does not resist when he drags her off the porch, into his house, by her hair. Instead, she flexes her body into him like a dancer on a pole. I stay flat on my back. My neck still burns from the hot pepper where Vida's lips touched my skin. When they're finally gone, I do it. Un poquito, just a little bit, I cry.

It's late. I'm lying face up on my bunk, one hand over my heart, waiting for her, in the dark. I got the bill of my hat pulled low. My eyes are wide open, though, gaze pinned to the bottom of Vida's bunk from below, as if I might miss her getting back unless I keep looking.

Finally, I hear the door open. I don't know if I should pretend to be asleep or say something. But then, she's there, next to me, in my bed. She nudges me. Move over, she whispers. I shimmy toward the wall. She turns her backside toward me, fitting her edges perfectly up against the angles of my front. Then, she lifts my arm and wraps it around her waist, tucks my hand under her hip, as if she's buckling herself into a car seat. Her chin is tucked into her chest when I hear her quiet sobs.

I don't ask questions. I don't need to. She trembles when I touch the bruise on her face. I feel what he's done to her in my own bones when she cowers as I cover her with my sweatshirt, tensing her belly when I situate my arm. Lying with her, I wish I was prettier than her so it could be me who has to take it from him. So I could've saved her. But she is so damn pretty. Too small and too pretty. I'm not the one he wants.

Suddenly, I prop myself up. I want to take you somewhere, I say.
Where? she says, still crying.
Get up.
Wiley, it's late.
Vámonos.
We'll get caught.
He won't hear us leave. Ándale.
Promise?
Promise, I say. *Lo prometo, I say, I say. I promise.*

We're standing on the tracks. Her two feet on one railway track, mine on another, facing one another. We're in the train tunnel. Abandoned tracks. My surprise for her. Our sounds vibrate, echoing like they'll never end. Sounds that are colors of the underground, colors of all the unknowns come to tag their names, to tell somebody (*no one can hear you*), anybody (*keep your voices down*), that they exist (*you are invisible*). A million tags in neons overlaying the others, each one scrubbed, ghosted to make space for the next, for another, to rise. When I hug her into me, I see HOPE in green, graffitied on the tunnel's curve behind her. I could sit her down inside the O, I think, I think, She'd be safe there, inside HOPE. Instead, I hold her. I whisper into her shoulder.

How long has he been hurting you? I ask.

The whole time.

Did you try to tell someone?

No. I been in worse homes.

My caseworker, Ms. B. I can call her.

I just have to get enough money to get out.

You don't have to keep taking that shit from him. El cabrón, I say.

I'm eighteen now. I can leave as soon as I have enough, she says. I think about her stash under the mattress. Seems to me it's not nearly enough to get herself out of there. Then she says, You know, he's not going to let you stay in the house, Wiley. After what you did.

Lo sé. I know. I know. We could leave here, together, I say. Tú y yo.

She's quiet then. I look toward the open end of the tunnel behind her. I'm certain she can see the other end, wide and free, beyond me. Two ways to get out. We're in the middle, on the tracks. Safe from the rain when it begins to fall. Drops are like footsteps— like the pitter-patter of ghosts—on the ground above our heads. She pulls away from me, gently.

She sits on the side of the tracks, her back rounded against the tunnel. Her elbows are on her knees, head hanging down. The air is thick from the heat in the tunnel, wet from the rain outside. I walk to her. There's an angel behind her painted on the tunnel wall, all white, outlined in black. It's kneeling, hands together at the chest in prayer. The angel is perfect. I look down on Vida. She's perfect. She's crying. I look away. Up. No face. The painted angel has no head.

I take her hands to pull her up. I guide her to the middle of the tracks to show her the angel. Then, in my backpack, I find the can. Gloss Banner Red. I close up on the tunnel wall where the angel is. She watches while I tag her name in big bold letters—VIDA—across the blank spot where the angel's head would be. I hold her hand. We face her name.

Everyone I've ever loved has died or left me, I say, I say, I don't want to leave you, I say.

If you stay, it will get worse for me.

But I love you, I LOVE YOU, I think, I think, *Te amo, mi Vida*, I do not say. I think about my mama, then. My mama died with a needle in her arm. That's what they say. They say. Say. *Say nothing, Wiley. Act right. Maybe this will be the one where you stay.* Abuela told me once that Mami said I came out her womb frowning with a full head of tight black curls. Didn't make a peep. Not a cry, not one sound at all. She said Mami loved me. I look at Vida. I think about how, before her, the only love I've ever known was that of ghosts.

I always wear it on my pointer finger. Abuela's ring. In the light at one of the tunnel's ends, I take it off. I slip the ring into Vida's hand, close her palm around it.

Use this to get out of here, I say. It's worth something.

Walking back, she sings to me *Oh! Susanna*, so softly, the only sound against cicadas and stars, and I hum along to hide my cry.

At the house, she drops my hand to unlock the gate, then closes it tight behind her. I say, Happy birthday. *I will never forget, I say, I say. Lo prometo.*

♛

I'm on the porch smoking. Ms. B's on her way. Only took her one week to place me in another home after el señor made the call. *I knew you'd ruin this, Wiley. What did I tell you?*

During my last week in the yellow house, Vida's eyes tell me to go by how she looks *past* me, how she already has her shoes on when he comes for her again, how she stays standing, rounded in her body, hands down her pockets, waiting for him. She doesn't say a word. Doesn't stall or shift. He doesn't have to call on her either; she's already walking toward him.

The last time I see her, she slips the ring off her pinky—the gold band I'd given her when we were safe on the tracks. She sets the ring on the small table beside our bunks. I never told her how long I'd worn it, since before the system, before all this. I'd worn it on a chain around my neck as a kid—from home to home—until I was old enough for it to fit a finger. By the time the door shuts behind her, the ring is still teetering.

I close my eyes, still have the burn of Vida's lips on my skin. Us two. After one kiss. My bottom bunk. Me wrapped around her from behind. Blowing across those welts in handprints on her cheeks. Se siente bien, she said, feels good, feel so good. I leaned into her forehead, her tears wetting my chin, our hands—four into one—gripped together between us at our chests.

Maybe, I should've left the ring for her. I didn't. Pero, entiéndeme por favor—you have to understand—I couldn't. Instead, I put it around my own finger. So I could remember she was no fantasma.

Vida is here, see, she's around my finger, real as gold.

I put my smoke out, tip my hat back. I nod toward Ms. B as she's rushing up the porch toward me. Next house is in Long Beach. I wonder what color it will be. In my mind it's blue. I imagine what I'll say to the next girl I share a room with—I should say, I will take the top bunk. No hay problema. I like to sleep closer to the stars. I wonder if she's ever been loved or left before. I wonder, should I warn her?—¡Cuidada! Beware!—love can get made in these colorful houses. Then disappear. Faceless, like a ghost.

WHAT MY MOMMA KNOWS
IS TRUE

MOMMA SAYS THAT my little fingers are like sausages. When she tells me this, my nose inches real close and I giggle when I smell bacon. I know my fingers don't smell like bacon for real, but it's funny how my mind always thinks they do whenever Momma says it. She says lots of things that come true fast. That's one thing about my momma—she seems to make things real just by saying so. It's like magic. I remember when I learned this about her because it was just last year when I turned six. And now I notice it all the time.

So when the glass elephant is dropped into my hands, I think it might be the grease of my sausage fingers that makes it slip and slide and drop, plunk onto Granma's thick pea green carpet. I am shocked because I feel a pain shoot through my body like the elephant would feel. But the bushy carpet buries it and I don't even hear the thud. I try to jump from the cushion of the couch cloud, but my bottom is stuck in between the crack. I wiggle and squirm and finally my feet find the ground. I am a fish with my fins flipping through the carpet and I can't see them; that floor is so furry and then, phew, I find it. Not with my eyes, no, but with my pudgy little fingers. The shiny black elephant is safe, and I cradle it like a baby doll. I feel a tear in my eye because I thought she was lost in that sea for all time.

I sit down where I am safe. On the plaid couch that eats my bottom. I hold the elephant nicely and wipe the tear away with the back of my hand. I look at my momma cause she is sitting in front of me, waiting. She is waiting to talk to me. Most probably to talk to me about something she knows. I can feel this is serious because what Momma says comes true and we both know this. Uncle Jerry and Poppa also know this. I think about it because the whole family is here and that only happens on birthdays or other special days. I wonder if it's my momma's birthday and I feel sad that I maybe forgot a special present for her. But then I think that there should be cake in Granma's kitchen for a birthday and there is not. So I know that it's not Momma's birthday. I am glad I did not forget about her.

Ebbie, do you want to keep the elephant you gave Granma? Momma asks me. The question pokes at the quiet room where Poppa stands smoking his cigarette near the kitchen doorway. Uncle Jerry looks at me. It seems he is waiting, too, but I don't really know why.

I love the smooth, heavy, glass black elephant. It feels like a soapy bath that my momma runs for me at night. She puts bubbles in the bath and makes it really hot so that I have to sit on the side of the tub and be scared to put my toes in. I always tell her that it's hot, but she tells me to put my toe in and count to three. She promises me that if I am brave enough to get to three, the water will not feel hot anymore. I do this and every time my momma's words come true. The water feels like a cozy blanket and I slide in until my nose sits on top of the big bubbles. Each time I know that I am brave and that my momma is right about what will happen.

The elephant's edges are round and its long trunk is silly but strong. It is as hard as the stones on the sides of Granma's house but is so good to feel with my fingertips. I found it to buy for her two years ago when the family took a vacation in the station wagon together. I don't remember where we went, but I am sure my momma would know. I also don't remember where the photos that Momma shows me of the beach and the sun are from. The only thing I really remember is riding in the car home because we went straight to Granma so I could give her the elephant. I am not sure if Granma knows that elephants are my favorite animal. I like them so much because their name starts with E just like mine does. E for elephant. E for Ebony. But I do know that Granma loves this elephant so much because it came from me.

No, Momma. I don't wanna keep it! The elephant is Granma's. She would be so sad to lose it. We can't take it away! I yell this. I feel angry at Momma for thinking about taking Granma's gift away. She needs the elephant to always remember me.

Ebbie, there is something I need to talk to you about. It is important and it is something I know is true, so it is time that I tell you. I always tell you the truth, right?

Yes, Momma. You do. I know you do.

Good. You trust me and I trust you. So I am going to tell you something that you have to promise me you will trust is true. You will not understand it right away, but you will come to understand it in time. I promise you this. Momma looks straight from her eyes into mine. I can see the line that connects us right there in the air. She is seeing inside me.

I feel a rush of heat up in my curly black hair. It feels like there is a fire up there and if I had a mirror, I think I would see that my ears are red. I am fiery and hot. My heart thumps around in my chest and my sausage fingers are slippery with sweat. I am afraid that Momma is mad at me and I try to remember if I said something naughty on the playground that Mrs. Apple told her about. I feel trouble creeping in all around me like when nighttime comes and I can't get sleepy. Then I remember that Momma asked me to trust her, like when I can't sleep and she tells me to practice the letters I learned in sign language. She promises me that this will make me sleepy and every night, when I am scared of not finding my dreams, I realize more that what she says is true. I remember this and it waters the fire in my head. I pet Granma's black, lovely elephant and I feel better so that I can hear my momma. I want to know what she knows is true.

Do you remember a little while ago when I told you Granma was sick, Ebbie? Do you remember that I told you it was different than a runny nose or a scratchy throat?

Yes, Momma. I remember. You told me that Granma was sick but that I might not notice because she is so strong. You told me that she will never talk to me about it because she doesn't want me to worry and because if she talked too much, there would not be as much time for her to play with me. Then you told me it was important for me to know, even though Granma didn't want me to, so that one day I would understand better what was most surely gonna happen, I say. I am proud because I think I remembered right. The sides of my mouth curl up, but the house with my family inside isn't happy that I'm starting to smile. So I don't.

Then Momma says, Well now is the time that I talked to you about. This is the time for you to understand better, but you must trust me that you will not understand it all. And that's okay. Two tears, not one like I had before, are crawling down my Momma's face, and she catches one in a Kleenex cupped on her lap.

Today is the day when Granma will go away. She is done living with us here in this house and you will not play with her like you usually do each day. Things are going to change because Granma is leaving us and today we must each say goodbye. This is why your uncle and your cousins and your Poppa are here together. We are together to say goodbye and you must try to understand just enough so that you can say goodbye, too. You will miss Granma when she is gone, but you will never be alone and you must trust me that this is true, she says. Momma is very sad now, too many tears to catch, and I try to put all my thoughts and feelings where they are supposed to go, but there are too many and they get lost in my mind somewhere I cannot find them. I understand right away that Granma is dying. But I am so, so mad because I do not understand why.

Maybe that mad feeling makes me remember. I remember. I remember. It was so long ago, way back when I was only five, a real little baby. I can tell how much I've grown when I think about how much less I knew back when I was a little girl. I'm a big girl now because of what I know, but it is hard not understanding adult things. I remember when I was mad at Granma, sort of like I am mad right now, and Poppa's car was bouncy and my head slapped the top of the Jeep cause my feet were too tiny to hold me down. We bobbled down the driveway and the blocks of salt made scratchy noises against the metal in back. I couldn't wait to grab Granma's big hand. She always held my sausage fingers tucked in tight so the tips stayed warm. She didn't wear the wig on those walks of ours, just a pretty silk scarf tied in a knot behind her ear. She looked so silly, my Granma, just like Poppa with little loose hairs dancing around his round head. I ran fast from the truck and I threw the screen door away from me and yelled, Granma, Granma, Granma! The deer are gonna love these blocks today … Granma! …

Granma? Where are you, Granma?

I couldn't find her in the normal spots: near the window with a big thick book, in the kitchen rolling the chicken parts in flour, in the bathroom cleaning her fake teeth. I couldn't find her. I was mad then like I am now, cause I don't understand what I should already know.

The house seemed as mad as me cause the stairs squeaked as I ran up to her bedroom, and I found her in the weirdest place to be when the sun was shining—in the room, in the bed, swallowed up whole by the pillows and covers. I scrunched my face up and when that smell tickled my nose, my yell broke something heavy and hushed in the room.

Granma. I said it just like that, plain. She rolled over. It sounded like her throat hurt cause it squeaked out when she told me that I had to go ahead without her.

In the end, Poppa had to help me lift the blocks out of the truck and lay them out in the yard so that the deer could lick 'em up. He didn't hold my hand and that made me even more mad and I didn't care whether the deer were happy or glad cause Granma wasn't there.

I am growing up very, very way too fast cause I wish now that I had not gotten mad when Granma was too sick to help me with the salt blocks. Wishing for something else seems like a very grown-up thing to do.

Now, I shift my bottom out from the crack of Granma's couch cushion and stand up. I hold out the heavy elephant, straight out to the world. I shout at each of them, Well, no one can have this elephant because it is Granma's and if Granma doesn't keep it I am going to throw it away. I am going to give it to the deer to carry away into the forest because none of you can have it. It's not yours and it's not mine. It's hers!

Saying this makes me run. The bathroom door slams—bang!—and shuts them all out away from me. I don't want them looking at me. I don't want to see my momma's face so sad and puffed up. I hug the elephant tight and crouch in the corner near the potty, the tightest corner I can find. Tears burn down my cheeks so hot, too hot, they burn.

It is quiet all around me. I cannot hear Momma or Uncle Jerry or Poppa or the cousins outside the door. I cannot hear anything but the trickle—drip, drip, drip—of the sink. I am sleepy but wide awake, afraid of finding my dreams in the corner of Granma's bathroom while she dies upstairs. So I stand up with an ache, still holding Granma's ... *my* soft, black, glass elephant. I find the mirror through the smudgy light in my eyes. I stand there looking at myself and all of a sudden, I see her behind me.

Granma reaches for my head and pulls the comb slowly through my frizzy black hair. She tells me that my hair is as naughty as I am sometimes and giggles when she kisses my cheek. She drags the comb hard backwards and gathers each clump of hair in her fist to hold it all together in one thick bunch. She combs and pulls and combs and pulls until the hair is smooth against my head. I gaze at myself in the mirror. My eyes look wider and the sides of my head throb from the stretch, but it feels so good. It pulls me together all tight and sturdy. Granma looks so happy, there above me in the mirror. I am warm when she touches me. I blink and look, blink and look. Then she is gone, but I can still feel her hands on my shoulders and her kiss, still sloppy on my cheek. She is gone but she is still here.

I turn the doorknob of the bathroom very slowly. The squeak is the loudest thing I hear because it is so quiet and dark in the house. Momma is waiting for me right outside the doorway and I crawl deep into her arms, leaning against her chest when she hugs me tight. Momma doesn't say anything to me because she knows I am ready. My momma knows me.

My hand is resting in hers and the elephant is tucked nice and tight into my other arm. I will not let it fall again. The stairs up are long and each one is harder for me to climb. But I get there, right up to the door of Granma's room and I smell that something sour. It makes my nose tickle again and I do not want to go in because I am afraid. But I trust my momma and I am brave. She lets go of my hand and I slide into the room.

Granma is lying very still with her covers tucked all around her. She looks like a butterfly before it pops out of its cocoon. Two pillows are under her knees and I see them poking up. Her eyes are closed and it is dark in the room, so I know she is trying to find her dreams. I wonder if she is practicing her sign language letters or if I should show them to her. I tiptoe to the edge of her bed and slide my sausage fingers under the blanket toward where I think her hand might be. I want to touch her hand but I cannot see the way so I feel around for it. With my other hand I set the lost elephant right next to her on the table. I let it go and I find her hand.

Granma's eyes open slowly. She finds me in the dark room but moves very little. She smiles at me and I feel proud again.

Ebbie, my dear, I love you very much. I will always remember you and I will always need you. Granma's words are scratchy and soft. She says, You are my favorite, dear, of all the children, of all the people I have known. You will never be alone because I will always be near you.

The shiny, round, soft, black elephant is staring at me. I can't quite find Granma's eyes in the dark room, but the elephant's eyes are sparkling and so I see them bright. I never looked so long at the glassy elephant eyes and for a second I forget about Granma because she is so quiet and thin. Right now I swear that Granma is looking at me right through those elephant eyes! I feel the life of it and then Granma's hand slips right out from under mine, just like that.

I want to find her hand again. But it's time to let go now, I can feel it. I drag my hand slowly out from under the covers and go toward the door. I look away from the elephant on the table and look for my Momma after I cross over and she is there waiting for me.

I do not understand all of this but I trust my Momma cause everything she says is true. I am not alone. She told me so.

UNDER HER CELLOPHANE SKIN

THAT GIRL THERE. With an empty bottle in a brown paper bag at her side. She's missing. Been reported by her father. Legs wide, sprawled on a blue plastic tarp under the overhang of Union Gospel Mission, the men's shelter down from the 7-Eleven, up against Skid Row. She's been spare-changing around Pioneer Square all morning. Did well enough to have nodded out by noon, chin resting against her chest. This is her usual spot.

On the street, a rush of warmth comes over the girl. She's sheltered by an old man standing above her. He unzips his jacket—the one given to him upon retirement from the UW Science Department—royal purple with a UW emblem on its sleeve. He slides his arms out, then gently edges the girl's limp body forward to lay the jacket around her shoulders. Next, he reaches through the cuff of one sleeve to catch hold of her hand, feeding her arm through, as if clothing a child in winter. After he's finished tending to her arms, the man zips her up. Now, she's cocooned in the jacket with sleeves hanging way past her hands, concealing the rig that had fallen loose from her arm.

Now, a sightseer, shuffling along to tour the Seattle underground, almost trips over her soiled legs. Nonchalant locals rush by the girl as if weaving around traffic cones. The homeless here are like streetlights or signposts, forgotten city fixtures. One passerby says, God loves you, then tosses a handful of coins at the girl's feet. Months living on Seattle streets. West Coast Heroin is stronger than back home. They call it Hero on these streets, and she loves this, how Hero takes you over like Spider-Man does Peter Parker. The girl feels cradled in her coma, protected. Her Hero has conviction, gets her having visions during daylight hours. She swings from webs, walks on water. Hero helps her see the truth of things. It's all so beautiful, really, like gliding across the gates of heaven.

Today, Lemon sees her sister way up there, hovering. Lucy wears a summer dress, no ... a nightgown, white cotton, with tiny berries embroidered along the collar ... berries at each buttonhole down the front ... berries along the dainty elastic edges of both ruffled cuffs. Her tangerine hair is washed and combed, sweeping through puddles along the street below her, wet and gathered at the ends like a paintbrush. Her feet are bare and unscathed as an infant's. She's *alive* and serene ... beautiful, clean. Then Lucy is right above Lemon on the street, and she whispers so close, so close, so close, she says, Don't forget you are fuchsia under all that black. Lemon tries to touch her face, but the angel's body shrivels, turns in on itself, like a snail to salt, and suddenly, she's tasting the hardened creature on her tongue.

In front of her now, the old man bends to pick up the coins scattered around the girl. He sets them in a neat pile beside her, then tunes his old AM/FM radio headphones. Jackson Browne, yes, that's it. Over the hood that's come down around her eyes, he places the headphones thoughtfully, like a tiara. Then, in a wave inside herself, Lemon feels her father here. Turning out the light beside her childhood bed, drawing the covers up toward her chin. Her father molds the edges of her small body until she's completely swaddled in soft down so that only her face shows, and he can kiss her forehead and say, Close your eyes, Lemon. Go to sleep now, my girl. I love you.

The song softens, muffled by her matted red hair as the old man leaves her in a whole other place with music suctioned to her ears. *Running on empty* ... a place of dusk and childhood on the Mississippi with her father. *Running blind* ... on the river's edge, she played house with the worms he used as bait, off a fly rod, when bugs jittered on the water around her father's waders, at sundown, in curdled amber light. *Running into the sun* ... she'd name them— the worms—for all the imaginary friends who gave her the kind of safe love she never could find in real life. One time, her father caught a baby turtle rather than a fish, and the girl cried until he proved to her that the turtle was still alive. *But I'm running behind* ... and off the turtle went upriver. Off the girl went, with her father. On the street, here she comes now. She's making her own way back.

Next, a lady in heels clips the girl's bashed up knee with her shoe's spike, then throws a buck on her lap. The pain to her knee gets the girl. She shoots up from the street, sharp like a needle. There's froth from her mouth all down her front and tangled up in the ends of her hair that's fallen out from under her hood. Her face is the same shade as a bloated Seattle sky that holds water like a fresh cadaver. The whole gray mess makes misshapen shadows across her face.

Lemon stumbles to standing. Hey, I don't need your fucking money, she slurs at the lady's backside as she walks away. Lemon wipes her mouth with the cuff of her sleeve. All around her she feels her father, the scent of English Leather. Had he been here? She crumples the lady's bill and stuffs it down the pocket of the jacket. Smells like home. Maybe he would know where to find his daughter? Her headphones are crooked, now covering only one ear. She looks like a beaten dog.

Obviously, you do, the woman says, spinning on her heels back toward her. She extends another bill. Lemon looks this one in the eyes. They're not turned down or sullen. No, it's not pity Lemon sees. This woman's wide eyes are hateful. She's angry, disgusted. Just take it, she says. Get off this street for a day. Go get yourself some coffee or something.

Lemon snatches the money from the lady's hand. Fuck you, she says. I mean, thank you, then bows like a court jester.

Better yet, get a *fucking* job, the lady says walking away, heels clicking against the street.

Her bottle's empty. Her Hero's up and vanished. She unzips the jacket, slides the headphones around her neck. Where did this shit come from? she wonders, then checks her pockets for what's left. Not even enough for a pint. Lemon craves Whiskey like having another lover on the back burner. She loves the taste of it and its deep wooden color like maple syrup. She loves the way Whiskey enters her and turns her into an entirely different kind of lady— a proud lioness, all balls and brazen, and … visible. Fuck the world! Fuck it all, Whiskey roars, and the girl comes out of herself completely. Whiskey says, You are *not* transparent. You are *not* homeless, kid—these streets are yours. You *are* the world, Whiskey shouts. She likes to sing on Whiskey, fuck on Whiskey, fight on Whiskey. There's nothing Lemon would refuse to do high on Whiskey. Unless it required her to leave the bottle behind. That's why the two brawled today—Lemon and Space. When Space told her, Find me some damn motherfucking money, Lem. I love you, baby, you know I do, but this shit's gonna get real *in your face* if you don't figure out how to make us some money, it didn't take Lemon more than two seconds to slap him right in the mouth. How dare you, Lemon said. I am not your slave, while Whiskey added, Go fuck yourself, under its breath.

The girl's lost all sense of time. And Space. Where the fuck is he? She makes her way to the 7-Eleven, pissed and sick. She's been running with Space since leaving Minneapolis on a Greyhound bus in the middle of the night on a ticket she'd bought with stolen cash from her father's wallet. Space had a handle of cheap whiskey he offered to share with her from two seats behind. Soon enough, he had shifted into position beside her. Lemon offered him Xanax from a bottle prescribed to her mother, and off they went, in and out of love and consciousness by the time they hit the North Dakota state line.

Space measured his blackouts in distance. Twenty-six-hundred miles, he told Lemon, all the way to West Virginia on a Greydog. Can you believe *that*? he said. I never was no good at sports growing up on the Tulalip Res ... but *drinkin*? He tipped his face toward her and whispered, Well, drinkin' I can win at *every* time. When he arrived in West Virginia, Space said he'd had no clue whose idea it had been to go all that way. It didn't matter, he said. All he needed to know was that he loved her—the tourist cowgirl with long legs and blond hair he'd met late one night while working at the Res casino. And he did, he said, he *did* love her. Which, to Lemon, seemed plenty enough for him.

At the time, Space's ramblings during that ride seemed important, as if she should write the information in ink on the back of her hand. A cheat sheet for later to prove she really knew him. Like how his real name was Shelton. Mama named me after Chief William Shelton, can you believe *that*? he said. Only ever been the chief of two things in my whole dang life: drinking and making love. Space grabbed his crotch with one hand, took a swig off the bottle with the other. Turns out, his West Virginia woman named him Space. For what's between my ears, he said. Then he laughed. He only laughed that one time the whole ride with Lemon. The other thousand miles Space cried and cried and cried some more, one fat tear after the next, tumbling from eyes behind mirrored glasses that he never—not once—removed, even in the dark.

He cried about how after a year of bliss in the West Virginia countryside, his woman kicked him out of their trailer after finding him ass up with her younger cousin which, he explained, was completely unavoidable given how she came on to him like that. Like what? Space went on, With her bare titties spilling right out her shirt and onto my face! Almost poked my eye out and just like that—BAM!—there I was with them things in my mouth. She sure as hell knew better than to leave them two alone, he said, especially with a handle of Southern Comfort on a Sunday. Then he said, I will probably end up loving you, baby girl. But know right now, I am not built for fidelity. And there was this giant of a man— a staunch Snohomish in steel-tipped cowboy boots with elegant sloping features and a black bandana holding back his thick long hair—heartbroken, like a toddler in timeout.

She meant to keep going west, all the way to the northern border. She doubted her parents would go as far as Canada to find her. The night of Lemon's departure, her mother had insisted on dinner together, the three of them. Lem, come on down. I made meatloaf, your favorite, her mother shouted up to her. The last of her Heroin, barely enough to keep her well, had just been shot into a vein on her foot from a needle she stored in a tin box at the back of her underwear drawer. Lemon imagined her mother's hands kneading raw meat in a glass bowl, red flesh gunked between each knuckle. Murderer, her mother would be thinking about her daughter, as she scraped the meat from each finger. She'd chop onions, the sting of loss oozing from her burning eyes. Meatloaf for the murderer. She wondered if the small things reminded her mother most of what the surviving twin had done. How rotten she really was.

Vanishing twin syndrome. Third trimester. One girl flattened in the womb, then absorbed by the other. That's how her mother said the young intern had described the condition, as if forecasting the lives of both girls by the death of one. The Heroin made Lemon imagine the young doctor as excruciatingly handsome when he delivered the news, dressed up in a fancy suit like a TV weatherman would wear. Heroin, her Hero. He'd have a wide veneered smile, pointing here, gesturing there. Hero-in. He'd say, In Minneapolis tomorrow, expectant mother, Charlotte, will mourn a fetus papyraceus while the temperature rises to new heights in the Martin family home with the experience of excruciating turmoil. The heat will eventually come down, temporarily cooled by severe intoxication of all family members, but this is to be followed by massive floods of tears and rage, so don't make life plans just yet. Hero. That doctor along with her sister would take up residence in the crackhouse of her muddied mind like relentless squatters. Lucy, painted in abstract each time she closed her eyes, reduced to a piece of wilting fruit wrapped in a filmy skin like cellophane. But her Hero. Hero made *everything* better. Cartoonish and impermanent.

Not tonight, Mom. I'm not hungry.

Nonnegotiable, Lem. Come down, her mother said.

Lemon dragged herself to standing. Fuck, she said. The girl knew she was wearing her mother thin. Just last summer, her parents finagled a job for the girl working for Les Hamlin, an old family friend, who Lemon forever associated with forced hugs and bad breath. On family holidays, he'd pull her into him way too close and hold on, forcing her to squirm out from under his large arm. She'd be the counter clerk at his deli, Hamlin's Ham & Stuff. The marquee alone made the girl want to vomit. You need some structure, Lemon. The routine will be good for you, her mother said.

She made it through her first few shifts. Then, a week in, her Hero ran out on her, and she hadn't been paid yet. She knew exactly what to expect being forsaken by her Hero. At the register, when her bowels began to clench she doubled over, crippled, intestines knotted so tight they could haul a semi. Jolts of pain from the nerves travelled down her limbs, made her legs throb then twitch like lit firecrackers. Withdrawal was a slow torture, like being skinned alive. She asked Mr. Hamlin for permission to use the restroom. In the stall, she hailed Mary, promised God, and negotiated with the Devil, just to make it through the day. Better yet, kill me, just do me in, here and now. Reflected in the mirror, she saw a monster. Her wasted arms braced her body with bent elbows that looked like little wings. The girl stared into dark eyes like holes in the sunken canoe of her face. She splashed herself with cold water and returned to the register. Then, when Mr. Hamlin's back was turned, she dumped the tip jar into her apron and ran for the door. When she returned home later that night, Hero in hand, her mother was waiting for her after a phone call from Mr. Hamlin. Lemon wasn't shocked.

These are the times I wonder what would've happened if Lucy had made it. I am so *disappointed* in you, the mother said.

Of course you are, Mom. It's hard to be the perfect twin when the other twin is *dead*, the daughter said.

Before going down for their last dinner together, Lemon boxed her paraphernalia carefully and stuffed the tin toward the bottom of the one backpack she'd take on the road. Her father sat at the head of the table across from her mother. An empty seat, always the same, faced Lemon. She pushed meatloaf around her plate with a spoon, droopy eyes on the blank spot across the table that was supposed to be her sister. Her mother drank two glasses of red wine, sips against silence. Lemon's father went on to talk about his day as if trying to bury the absence in the room. Her mother drank more. The girl felt them watching her with suspicion, like a trainer watches an unfed tiger. She knew they were never sure of what she'd do. Lemon's stomach turned at the pink grease on her plate. I'm done, she said. Then, she shoved back from the table, leaving her mangled meatloaf behind.

Later that night, she sat on the carpeted stairs leading to their second floor to eavesdrop on a discussion between her parents. Her father's voice was low and collected, rational. Her mother's words were slow and slurred, but she was always was the louder of the two. This sloppiness would make stealing the Xanax on Lemon's way out all the more possible.

I found an empty bottle of booze underneath her bed, Rod. It's like she wanted me to find it, she said.

She's a teenager, Char. I mean come on. You're being dramatic.

She's nineteen, an adult. I can't do this anymore. I'm afraid for her. I think we need to consider getting her some help.

We've tried that already, her father said.

Of course they're afraid, Lemon thought. *I'd be afraid of me, too.*

Her mother's voice got softer then. Lemon crept down to the bottom stair to listen closer. I wonder about the two of them, her mother said. If Lucy would've been like this, too, had she made it out of my fucked up womb to see the light of day. Lemon's just not right, Rod.

The pills, Charlotte. Lemon could hear him shake the bottle at her. Just stop with these. You're not making sense. None of this is your fault. It's not your body's fault or Lemon's or mine. The girl needs us. We have got to pull things together, here. You're not setting a good example for her.

And *you* are?

Lemon stopped listening to them argue then. She tiptoed back upstairs to finish packing her bag, considering how fitting, how truly tragic and ironic, the whole mess would become. She knows they'd think it was unnatural for her to leave without saying goodbye. In the end, it would all be right. She'd save them from the monster she was, help them salvage what remained between them as if refrigerating the leftovers of a perishing family. One twin, sweet, vanishes before birth. One twin, embittered, vanishes after. She shut the front door tightly behind her, careful to close it all the way. Then, she locked up and slid her key under the door for them to find later, after she was gone.

At the Seattle Greyhound stop, Space begged her to stay. Baby, please, look, you and me, we are like, what's that old movie? Bonnie and Clyde! You and me are like them. Then, he cried even more which absolutely disgusted her, coming down as hard as she was. When the bus left the Seattle terminal, Lemon watched its backside from a bench outside in the rain. Under a streetlamp, rainbows reflected off oil on the ground. Pacific fog mixed with exhaust rising from under the bus as it pulled away, northbound at midnight. Lemon smoked while Space rested his head on her shoulder. She finished the Whiskey. Two things comforted Lemon most about the man twice her age: his desperation, and not having to look in his eyes. The rest, she decided, she could deal with. Last she saw before her blackout was the butt of the bus and a child waving until the girl shrank into the size of a small baby doll, then disappeared around the road's next bend.

Now, she swears she'll strangle the life out of him if she ever sees Space again. Inside 7-Eleven, there's her favorite cashier, Kofi, distracted by the small TV behind the counter playing reruns of The Simpsons. At the counter, she slides a package of gummy bears into her pocket then asks, Kofi, you seen Space?

Lemon sunshine, you look good today, no? This show so funny. Kofi sucks on sunflower seeds, then spits each tiny shell into his hand. Swannies. Check there, he said.

Swannies. The one bar in Occidental Park that doubles her pour at lunchtime if she promises the bartender, Zeek, that she'll eat something. Jesuschrist, Lem, at least a fucking carrot stick or whatnot. App's on the house if it will keep you from what happened last time.

Last time? It was an *accident* for Chrissakes. Plus, Johnny Boy's the one who told her what happened after the fact, and he's completely unreliable. A regular daytime drinker with a wife and a couple kids. He told her he'd been laid off from Boeing recently. Seems to Lemon he's spending his days hiding out at Swannies. One time, he tried to stick his tongue down her throat right there at the bar. All she remembers is Listerine beneath the booze on his breath and the prick of his mustache against her upper lip. She still ended up in the stall with him that day for a line of blow off the lid of the toilet seat. When she took his coat off, she remembers thinking he smelled like the oldest guy she'd ever been with by a mile.

What *had* happened last time? Johnny Boy told her that she'd seized right there in the middle of the bar. There she was, she'd been told later, like a real epileptic, foaming at the mouth, bashing her head against the floor, her hands crippled like claws. Zeek and

Johnny, they swore to her they'd tried to help. And there was another guy there, too, Johnny Boy said. An old guy he'd seen around a few times. You know the one. Never drinks, just stares at a full glass. Yeah, that one, real calm like. He knelt beside her the whole time, cradling Lemon's head in his hands. His glasses slid down his nose, but he never let go, not once. When it was all over, the man placed her head on the floor like a jeweler sets a precious stone. Damn it, boy, he shouted at Zeek. Make yourself useful, and get me a wet rag. He smoothed the hair away from the girl's forehead and laid the rag across. Then, like nothing had happened at all, he went back to his stool. It was creepy, Lem. Like he knew you or some shit, Johnny Boy said. Lemon came out of the episode good as new, but she'd bitten her tongue, so for the rest of the week she lisped, her high voice sounding more like Mike Tyson than a white teenage girl with a Minnesota accent. She hasn't been back to Swannies since.

She opens the front door to the bar slowly. Zeek sees her first. Oh fuck, here we go, he says, wiping the bar down. It's too early for most customers, just a few daytime drinkers straggled along the bar.

I'm just looking for Space, man. You seen him? Lemon starts walking toward pool tables at the back.

Have a seat, Lem. Zeek pats his hand on the bar. Free pour, he says.

She sits. He sets a glass down and there's her beloved, her manly man, Whiskey, right from the bottle, with grooves like ripped muscles, a torn label that reminds her of Zoro. Whiskey winks while Zeek pours long and tall. Suddenly, all the world's edges seem softer.

Lemon drinks from her glass as if making love. In Johnny Boy's seat to her right, an old man stares through a short glass filled to the rim. No ice.

You gonna drink that? Lemon asks.

Your boyfriend left with a girl who wasn't you out the back door just as you walked in.

What'd you say?

You heard what I said. He's gone. You're better off without him.

Lemon looks to Zeek. Zeek shrugs, then pours her another.

How do you know who my boyfriend is?

I've been watching you. Been coming around here for a while.

Lemon picks up her glass and moves over to the stool beside the man. What do you mean, you've been watching me? You some kind of perv or something?

I'm too old to be perverted. Don't have the stamina for making trouble.

Well what then?

I saw you earlier today on the street. The jacket's a little big, but it ought to keep you warmer out there. The headphones are old. They're still good though. When I saw you, I thought you'd like to hear some music in your condition. My wife, April, used to stretch those very headphones across her belly when she was pregnant.

These are *yours*? She takes the headphones from around her neck and sets them on the bar in front of them. Then, she leans toward him. What is this, man? I'm not your project. You give me all your shit, like I belong to you. I'm not yours to fix, and I don't need your fucking charity.

Zeek walks over, lifts a bowl of nuts to run a rag down the bar. Come on, Lem. The guy's just trying to be nice, he says. This is the one that helped you out the last time you were here. Remember? He raises his eyebrows and sets the bowl down. Least you could do is be friendly. Zeek cocks his head toward the man.

That's what all perverts do, she says. They're all very *nice*. Lemon drinks, thinking of old Lester Hamlin and his long hugs.

No, it's just that you remind me of my daughter, the man says. How she might have been, that is.

How's that?

Beautiful. Red hair. With a fire in you.

I'm a mess. Never have done one good thing in my life.

At least you're alive. You're here. That's something.

Lemon looks at this man. He seems to be withering with the time taken to pass each moment. She thinks he might be dying, right here, in front of her. Then, he removes his wallet from his back pocket. Inside is a photo behind a plastic slot. He pries out the photo and sets it on the bar. When he caresses it, Lemon notices the skin on his hands, loose and wrinkled, his knuckles gnarled like knots on driftwood.

You can't save me, Lemon says. No one can.

I can try, he says. You must let whoever loves you *try*.

She drinks. The man's glass remains full and untouched. Then, he begins. He tells her about April, his dear. How he'd met her in summer on Vashon Island at the Strawberry Festival. From across the street at the parade, he'd seen her for the first time through a pair of wooden legs as tie-dyed banjo players stomped by on stilts. He tells Lemon about that wild tangerine hair of hers. How he'd smiled quickly when their eyes met, pretending he didn't know she was looking at him. How he'd watch April in silhouette, against low light, outside their RV—looking in, under California moonlight, when they'd parked under the stars overnight on their trip to Sonoma, wine country. How in the capsule of the RV, when she lifted her nightgown, her naked body brought a wash of sweetness and earth over him, like plums and pine. How they'd make love, and after, he'd prop himself on his bony elbow while she sat cross-legged, her books strewn about them. Then, she'd close her eyes and pick one out to read to him. Rumi and Neruda, lyrics from Laura Nyro or Joni Mitchell. He even told Lemon how his mother named him. That she'd said giving birth to him was like passing an ostrich through a keyhole, his long limbs and fingers, bony elbows and knees. *Not a soft spot on the boy*, she'd said. *That's why I named him Artist. To soften him up a bit.* And how when Art found April, his level, sensible mind curved. How she could coil his straightest angles. Art tells Lemon everything in one broad sweep. It's like he's ticking off an inventory and cleaning up what's left in back.

When he finishes, his face is still straight ahead as if he's boxed in a confessional and Lemon's the priest. She can't find anything shameful about it. These are the things people remember about love, Lemon thinks. Then, suddenly, she remembers sitting on the knee of her own father. Him holding her tightly at the waist, bouncing her while he sang *You are My Sunshine*, how close he'd lean to be nearer to her, how happy he seemed. Where's your daughter now? Lemon asks.

Art cups his hands around the full glass in front of him. He'd gotten too drunk the night of his daughter's birth, barely made it to the hospital in one piece. When he arrived, the baby was already crowning, and April was heaving her final push. When the daughter arrived, April softened completely, breaking open like a river rushing toward its falls. Art kissed his wife's head. But then, then, all was silent. There were no cries. The mother jolted toward the child. When April realized her baby girl was gone, she hardened solid, from a rushing river into ice frozen over. Her heart was shattered. The doctors had to pry the infant from her mother's stiff hands.

I haven't had a drink since, Art says. Not for thirty-one years. He runs his finger around the rim of his glass. When I found her in our bed a couple weeks back, I thought she was sleeping. Her cheeks were still pink, alive. We'd been married over half a century when she died. Now that she's gone, there's nothing much left to make up for. Art pulls the drink toward himself. He turns toward Lemon and looks in her eyes for the first time. Then he says, Making mistakes is not the same as being one. You are not a mistake, and you still have *time*.

Suddenly, from the back door, in comes Space. Hey, Lem, I been looking for you, baby. How you doing?

Lemon downs Art's drink and sets the empty glass down. She saunters over to Space as if Zoro himself. She slaps him, lightly, upside the head. Space brings his hand to his hair. He's got tears in his eyes. What the hell was that for? he says like a spanked child.

You know what that's for. I'm done with all this. And I hate when you cry. Then she turns to Art and says, It's not your fault, Art. It was never your fault.

Outside, she has to walk uphill, all the way to First and Pike to find a payphone. No cell, and hardly any cash left at all. She knows the phone number by heart.

Dad?

Lemon, is that you? Where have you *been*? My God, Lem, thank God, it's you.

Why'd you name me Lemon?

What? You know why, Lem. Where are you? Just come home. Or I will come get you. Tell me where you are.

Tell me, Dad.

Her father cries when he sings that old sunshine song to her over the phone. You always make me happy, Lem, even when skies are gray. His voice trails off as she pulls the receiver away from her face and sets it down on the hook.

She walks back down to Occidental Park where she sits on

a park bench—that one—the one from a month or so ago. When she was loaded from the Heroin and drunk on Whiskey. She carved an anarchy symbol in tiny scratches on the metal of the bench's backrest. She sits back and imagines the very back row of the Greyhound bus, the last seat, looking ahead, with rain hitting the windows behind her.

MOUTH ORGAN

IT WAS RIGHT close to August when they decided to give it another go. Mosquito season. Monk remembers suggesting a camping trip on the fly to the banks of some Midwestern river he's since forgotten the name of. They packed the hatchback of Gloria's Buick wagon as if winning a game of Tetris with no room to spare. Brought only last-minute necessities: two-man tent, single-burner camp stove, a couple wool blankets, and a pillow or two. A change of clothes for each tossed into a shared duffel. Monk had his harmonica, as always. Gloria brought her new 1980 Martin acoustic, he's sure—right, for campfire strumming, she'd said. And of course, her sheepdog, Puppy, never left behind, who jumped the back seat and made a nest of the blankets in the hatchback before they hit the first mile marker.

Gloria drove. His woman loved to drive. And Monk loved to watch her from the side. She wore cutoffs, her bare thighs buttered by the hot thick air. He kept a hand over her leg. She threaded her fingers over the top of his. They slid against one another, greased by the heat, touching the whole ride.

Monk turned up the radio dial. Gloria rolled her window down, all the way down. He sank back in his seat, she was propped against the door with her knee. He surfed the wind with his arm, she tapped her bare toes to their song. He put his dark shades on, she sang to him sultry and long. He drew his harp from his front shirt pocket, she kept time on the gear shift, knocking. He breathed, she sang, he blew, she kept on. His woman was so good. She was so good at just keeping on.

In the rearview was Puppy, the dog, lips blown back by the wind, tongue loose and free. All three, on the open road. Monk closed his eyes. He had felt free like this once, as a kid, before Pop left, before his mother soured like bad milk. They'd driven this same route, the old Lincoln Highway, in summer. Monk took the back, he remembered, where Puppy sat. When he laughed at Pop's stupid jokes, the hot air dried out his mouth. He remembered how when his parents began to argue up front, he'd closed his dusty lips with grit on his tongue.

Later that year, Pop cut and run with some lady his mother named Betty the Bimbo. After that, Monk's mother insisted she be called by her given name: Bunny. No more of this kid shit, Monk, and no more calling me Mommy. You're the man of the house now, she'd said. Bunny spent that whole school year in her nightgown, smoking one Pall Mall after the next. Until one day, Monk got home from school and Bunny had on a dress and a dainty apron tied around her waist. She'd reminded him of a paper doily all done up like that. She was cooking supper for a man she'd met at the Piggly Wiggly. That one down on Sheridan, Monk. You know, the fancy one. The two had met in the bread aisle when the man dropped a twelve-pack of Miller High Life cans and she came to his rescue, cradling the cans in her arms to carry them out for him. He remembers blushing seeing his mother so happy about that first one.

She called him Mr. Handsome. Really, he was a Mr. Brawny type, a burly man with a rugged beard who rode his Harley in from Chicago to shack up with her on the weekends. One time, Monk found Mr. Handsome's *Playboy* in the bathroom hidden between Bunny's *Better Homes & Gardens*. He thumbed through, skipping over the pages with words. The women with the pinkest nipples excited him most. When he found the centerfold, he tilted the magazine and the beautiful woman's long legs unfolded onto his lap. The crease ran directly across her belly. He smoothed her flat along his thighs. Suddenly, he could only think of Bunny positioned with Mr. Handsome. He dropped the magazine as if the thing was up in flames. Quickly then, he picked the lady up and folded her back in, head first, realizing that he was fully erect with only his mother on his mind.

Monk ran to his bedroom and slammed the door. He locked himself in. Frantic, he rummaged through his room and found the old harmonica Pop had left behind. The one he'd found in a cardboard box of things Bunny was set to give away. He ripped the covers back from his bed and jumped in. He pulled the sheet over his head, panting, his heart leaping like a bullfrog. With one hand, he held the harp to his mouth. He ran his tongue back and forth along the wood comb, he sucked and licked, caressing the back of the plate with one hand, the other hand rubbing himself down, while the harp wailed like a screeching cat. When it was all over, Monk slid the harmonica into his shirt pocket, just like Pop did, and patted it close up against his heart. Monk felt as if he'd reunited with a severed body part, like a long-lost limb or an extra organ.

That first Mr. Handsome bought Bunny a leather rider jacket and a black bandana. Even got a helmet with her name—*Bunny*—painted in red across the back and a little pink Playboy rabbit right below that. By the time summer rolled around, she'd perked up like a houseplant to water. By the summer after that, the helmet was bagged up, rolling around the trunk of her Lincoln Continental like a retired bowling ball alongside the leather biker boots she'd soon dump at the nearest Goodwill. Could've been Mr. Brawny's head in that bag for all the kid knew. Never saw the guy again. Monk began to call them Bunny's Honeys, all the men in and out. Only one guy stuck around; Monk still lived at home.

In the car, Monk lit a smoke. You want one, Glor? he asked.

Not today, she said. Take the wheel, would you? He loved that reckless move of hers, trusting him to steer. He kept his eyes on the road while she pulled her T-shirt above her head and threw it over his eyes. The smell on that shirt was earth and body, *her* body, all up his nose, ballooning around his head until his mouth watered. He threw the shirt back at her, aiming at her lap. There she was, in nothing more than her bra, one leg still propped against the driver door, her arm resting on her knee, hand surfing against the wind.

She laughed then, her free-falling gutsy bellow of a laugh, all teeth and spit and snorts. She'd come completely unglued, which never failed, always made him laugh, too. He'd never forget the first time he heard her like that, the night he met her, late, making the rounds with Frankie and Marz. As usual, they ended up at Redhead's, the piano bar on Ontario off the Blue Line. Real snazzy joint with strong drinks and fine women. They'd go there late on weeknights. When customers cleared out, the manager let the boys get on stage and play. Marz was behind the four-piece kit, Frankie on that fancy old Steinway grand, and Monk standing at the front, both hands cupped around the mic and his harp. They were just about to get going with their set when Monk noticed her.

Yo, Frankie, Monk said. Look at the new girl behind the bar.

Holy shit, Frankie laughed and downed a shot. She's fine, in a vanilla-suburb-kid kind of way.

You think she's a real redhead? Could be false advertising, Marz said and winked at Frankie. Monk knew it was a dare. She really wasn't his type. Too slight in the frame, auburn hair, emerald eyes. Fair-skinned and dainty like a baby bird. He liked Latin women the most, the ones who could roll their r's to him in bed, bronzed ones, round ones in the hips and behind. Mostly, he liked women all at once, not one at a time.

Only one way to find out, Monk said, throwing back his Jack on the rocks. He made his way to the bar, dropped onto the stool, and slapped a ten-dollar bill down. Laid his harmonica on top of the bill knowing she'd have to see it before she got paid. She barely talked to him at all when she served his drink, looked into his eyes the whole time. Didn't skip a beat at the harmonica either, just slid the bill out from under. Graceful, she was, and delicate, like a kite in the wind.

Anyone ever say you look like Bob Dylan? she'd asked. Monk wasn't surprised by her question. He had wild hair, a long nose, and deep almond eyes. The boys thought Monk played like him, too, could easily pass for his cover, especially when he wore his harp in a holder hanging at his neck. No, what surprised him was the *way* she asked him. It was the sound of her that brought Monk's chin to the ground. Her voice was like a tiger growl from the mouth of a kitten. The sexiest purr he'd ever heard.

What's your name?

Gloria. Who are you?

Monk.

How'd you get a name like Monk?

My pop named me. He loved jazz. Thelonious, Coltrane, Davis, you know. All that shit.

Do you?

Do I *what?*

Love all that shit.

I'm a blues guy. I'm better than that.

Better than what?

All that jazz.

Then, there it was, like lightning ... a brash belly roar that cracked through the whole joint like when a bowling ball hits pins. She reminded him of mist and thunder, all rolled into one. The boys had to pry him away from her to get on stage. Monk was stumped. She'd gotten him all tripped up.

When he finally got up there, Monk pulled out his harp, wrapped his fingers around its back side, eyes on Gloria. He licked his lips caressing the cover plate with his thumb, then put the harp to his mouth like a pacifier, snuggled right up against his lips. He knew every inch of that beauty by touch of tongue. His eyes softened as he closed them. He settled into *Just Like a Woman*, came down over the song like an umbrella, hunching his long back, leaning into his grip. He wagged one hand over the other so those first notes were long and soupy from the hammock of his hands. He swayed one leg in time with the slow rhythm as the boys played. His brow crumpled between his eyes like a paper fan, and his eyes rolled back as a tear spilled down his cheek. When he opened his eyes, Marz was in a roar beating on the drums while Frankie just shook his head down toward the keys. And there was Gloria, right next to him, her Martin acoustic hanging on a strap as she arched her neck up toward the mic. She leaned in so close to him that the air he gathered was partly hers. They were so tight, he tasted the cinnamon on her breath.

Monk stepped back away from the mic so he could watch her. Gloria finished the duet on her own while each hair on Monk's body stood in salute to the way she sang. Her voice was husky, as if from ages ago, and low—so deep and slow ... like molasses. From behind, her whole body moved like a finger through honey, and Monk felt so buzzed by her, it was as if she'd sucked him clean into her. They named the band Gloria and the Honeys. Monk's idea, but Gloria loved it. He could tell by the way she smiled.

He looked out beyond the open road, then at her while she drove. He'd been growing into his love for her as if filling out a bigger-sized shirt—slowly, without really trying. She made him feel more grown-up. Truth was, he'd surprised himself by staying wrapped up in her so tight for the past few months steady. She was young, a year younger than Monk, just eighteen. But she *looked* young, too, and smart, like some bookworm-type he'd find sitting under a tree in Hyde Park near campus. The women Monk dated were always older than him, late twenties at least. Sometimes he thought the band was what held them together.

Aren't you glad you decided to roll with me, Glor? Monk asked. She nodded and grinned, but he could tell she was still stung. Monk wanted to apologize to her, right then and there, for what went down between them the night before. He'd rolled up to her pad late, way past bar time, in Frankie's busted out Dodge van. Drunk as hell, they parked out front her apartment building, smoked a joint. He tried yelling for her from down below. She turned out her bedroom light. Next thing Monk knew, he was on the harmonica and Frankie had his guitar. Marz was banging out Bob Dylan's *Tombstone Blues*, slapping the wheel hardest when Daddy hits the alley looking for food. Then Monk made his way to the lawn and got down on all fours to serenade her. But he was more like a wolf than a man with raucous howling, being as high as he was, until neighbors' lights came on, and some even came to their windows, and finally, Gloria was forced to come on down.

She stood on the stoop in her pajamas. Puppy had followed her and sat at her feet. Both glared his way. I'm not sending you back to your mother's like this, so you can stay, she said. But just remember, you are not the ramblin' man you think you are.

He rolled onto his back, swaying his hands and feet up toward the sky. Come on Glor. I'm just blowin' in the wind, baby. I'm just blowin' in the wind!

No Monk. You're just a kid who still lives with his mother. And if you want me, you're going to have some growing up to do. And some settling down.

That was the closest to pissed Monk had ever seen her. In bed that night, he apologized by using what he'd read in the newest *Playboy* to try to get her off. She groaned like she was into it, but he could tell she was faking by her slack body. He peeked through one eye down on her, and there she was, staring up at the ceiling, lost in some kind of dream.

In the car, he couldn't find the right words by the time they had popped the tent, less than a mile down some trail off a frontage road leading to the river—hidden just enough by a thicket of sumac under a clump of old sugar maples. So close to the old Lincoln that drivers could probably hear them make love after bickering about which way to face the tent. He smoked a joint. She didn't want any. He remembers a dead leaf got stuck in Gloria's hair on its sail off the branch. A red-tailed hawk swooped down on their sunset campfire from the top of a white oak at the river's edge while Gloria sang to him right before Puppy got skunked. Frantic, the dog ran straight into the tent after being sprayed, fishtailed like a netted trout, trying to rub the scent off before rolling herself in their bedding like a taco. They slept on the sand dunes that night, along the river, while Puppy took the tent.

In the morning, on the sand dunes, Monk looked toward Gloria. He wanted to trace the outline of her profile with his finger, from the space between her emerald eyes, down the slope of her long nose, and dip into that perfect little divot above her upper lip. He smoked the roach. She lay belly-side up along the banks of the river, as they laughed at how she looked just like one more billowing sand dune along that stretch. How her belly's crest heaved when she breathed like the wind gathered dunes into waves. Auburn hair coiled down around her soft shoulder, just off to the side. Monk suddenly felt like he was on the set of some old romantic Western he'd seen as a kid with Pop where the cowboy rides off on horseback with the half-naked girl at the end. He still couldn't find the right things to say. Instead, he draped his arm across his eyes.

Monk, she said. I'm ...

I know, honey. Don't say it. It's my fault. I'm sorry.

No, she said, I'm pregnant.

He shot up so fast with fright, his favorite harp fell from his front shirt pocket, rolling like a stone to land square between them.

It was right close to noon when Gloria pulled up to drop Monk off at his mother's. They'd hardly talked on the drive back to the city, just a few words here and there. Monk filled the silence by breathing into his harmonica, barely took it away from his face. He grabbed every last item of his from Gloria's Buick, even checked underneath the seats. As he shut the door, he smiled at her, then waved. He felt like a clown at the end of the party.

Gloria leaned across to the passenger side and rolled down the window. When you stop wanting to wander, give me a call, she said. Until then, don't bother. Slowly, she drove off. As she did, Puppy hopped the seats to watch him from the rear window, panting ... no, smiling, he thought. He stood there, still waving, watching them as if through a peephole until they were gone.

Inside the house, Monk smelled Folgers and bacon, reminding him of his childhood. He patted his pocket to check for his harp and walked toward the smell of food. He imagined how it would be—to sit down at the kitchen table with Bunny. She'd pour him coffee and waltz around in her dainty apron tied around her waist. He'd watch her dance around the kitchen like she used to while she cracked eggs and waved a fork through the air like a conductor, whipping and whistling as the fork tinged against a glass bowl. She'd let him cry about Gloria and she'd listen to him—*Everything's going to be okay. Bunny's here, Monk*—while she sprinkled flour on a board, then searched for a rolling pin in the back of one drawer. She'd make him his favorite cookies. Then after, she'd wipe her floured hands down her front before smoothing his hair and wiping his tears and hugging him in, so close to her chest, he'd hear her heart beat and smell her sweat. He was beat.

Then, at the doorway of the kitchen, he saw them together, gathered around the breakfast table. Frankie, shirtless, looked down, buttering his toast. Marz was behind Bunny with his arm around her shoulders looking over her standing at the stove, their backs toward Monk. All three of them, in his kitchen, while he just stood there watching.

Frankie took a sip off the rim of his coffee cup. Hey man, you're back. Great, he said. We stopped by to jam. You down?

Bunny's the best, man. Marz spun around with bacon hanging

from his mouth. She made us this whole spread. You look beat, man. Where's Glor?

Monk let his duffel fall from his shoulder to the floor. He looked at Marz and shook his head. Then, Bunny turned toward him. Monk looked her up and down. She was in a black satin kimono with a full face of makeup and a lit cigarette stuck between her bright red lips. With an oven mitt on one hand, she held a frying pan with bacon still sizzling in grease off the heat.

She squinted through the smoke in her eyes. Sit, Monk. Have some breakfast with your boys and your dear old mommy Bunny, she said. Then she bent across the table toward Frankie to put the pan down. Her robe was tied so loose in front that when she reached forward, one breast spilled out the top of her red lace brassiere. She picked up a piece of bacon with her two fingers and dropped it on Frankie's plate. Then, she licked her finger and ruffled Frankie's hair. Eat up, cutie, she said. You're probably ravenous. She winked. Frankie tried to look away, but it was like being stuck in traffic with an accident ahead. No choice in the matter.

What the fuck, Bunny? Monk said. What's all this?

I'm just entertaining your guests, Monk. Pour me some more coffee, would you Marz, darling? She held her cup toward him.

I'll get up with you boys later, Monk said. Thanks for coming by.

You don't want to jam, man? Frankie asked.

Later, Monk said. Later.

Marz set the coffee pot down next to Bunny's cup. Frankie got up from the table. On the way out, he grabbed a piece of bacon, shoved it into his mouth, and kissed Bunny on the head. Thanks for breakfast, Bunny, Frankie said.

Anytime, sugar, she said.

As the boys made their way out, Bunny poured herself a cup

of coffee. She used a tiny spoon to add sugar, then stirred. Metal clinked the side of the cup. Monk walked over, sat at the table across from her, and took the spoon from her hand. He laid it down in front of her. Bunny wrapped the robe tightly around her middle and crossed her arms at her chest.

Look at me, Mother.

What do you want from me, Monk? I'm doing the best I can to get by.

You know the thing about you, Bunny, is that you're always trying to live someone else's life. I want you to stay away from my friends. Stay away from *my* life.

Your life? Your life is only yours because I gave it to you. Me, and me alone, kid. The way I see it, you owe me everything. Bunny balanced the tiny spoon between her fingers, pinky out. She heaped a spoonful of sugar. Holding the mound high, she tilted slowly toward her cup, eyes on Monk. I sacrificed so much of my own pleasure to raise you up decent, she said. I was nineteen when I had you, Monk. *Nineteen.*

I didn't ask you to stay with me, he said. I wish you would've left instead of Pop. Then, Monk bit his lip, hard, suddenly pained that he hadn't stopped himself. His shoulders curved when he looked down, tapping two tense fingers on the table.

Bunny stood then, slowly. She walked to the refrigerator. At its front, she moved one of a hundred magnets aside—a miniature Harley from Mr. Brawny—and brought the hanging photo to the table. She sat.

Remember, Monk, there are so many things that a kid never sees. I used to hear you crying late at night, after your father left. I'd stand at your bedroom door. Sometimes I'd fall asleep right outside listening to you cry.

But you never came in, he said. I was alone.

Bunny spun the photo to face Monk. And there they were, Pop in the background, a can of Old Style in his grip, and Bunny, holding baby Monk wrapped up tight to her chest and leaning in, bright red lips to his tiny bald head. She traced her fingers along the photo, ending on Monk's face as if he was the treasure on a map. The thing about being a kid raising a kid, she said, is that somehow you wind up fumbling around for a while being kids together. Then suddenly, you both have to figure out how to grow up.

You're no kid now, Bunny.

Neither are you, son, neither are you. When you figure out how it's all done, be sure to let me know. In the meantime, don't turn out like your father.

He wanted to say, *I'm better than him.*

He wanted to say, *You made me like this.*

He wanted to say, *I'm better than you.*

But instead, she said to him, I'm sorry, son. Then, she touched her hand to his and said, I could've been more like a mother. I could've done better. Bunny slid the photo toward Monk. Keep this, she said, to remember.

She looked up at him then, and he noticed how her eyes were almond-shaped just like his. He saw the curls in her hair and brought his hand to his own head. He wondered what his muffled cries sounded like from the other side of his bedroom door. He wondered how different her bed felt the night after Pop left her and how different it felt the first night she had someone else in it. He wondered what it was like to be her. He wondered what it would be like for him without her.

I'll just get changed and we'll have some coffee together. How about it, Monk? Bunny headed away from him, down the dim hallway toward her bedroom, as her kimono came untied completely, trailing behind her like giant wings on a moth.

When she was gone, Monk got up from the table and pushed his chair in. He walked toward the front door of their home. With his hand on the knob, he stopped. Then, he rushed back to the kitchen to pocket the photo. Outside, he took a breath before walking to the Blue Line. Off the porch, he carried the smells of his childhood with him in the fabric of his cotton shirt. Folgers and bacon, right up his nose the whole ride, stops and all.

Later, when Monk rang Gloria's buzzer, he suddenly wished he had played Bunny a song before he left. He would've played her the very first one he ever learned. He almost turned around then, to run back home. But then there was Puppy. And right behind the dog was Gloria. She was already on her way down.

LUCKY PENNY

CLEAVE WORKS THE graveyard shift at the Citgo station on Holton down by Usinger's sausage factory. He comes from a long line of Milwaukee meat and casings, each man a better butcher than the one who came before. Except Cleaver. He says he was never much good at willful killing. For Penny, this is something she's never forgotten about her man—his mercy.

He'd tried to get a job delivering for the factory but got passed up when the manager found a DUI on his record. Penny envies the way he works, the way he seems to love the simple things. She senses that the man may really love her, too. She sees it in his habits, how he secures things. Like when he double knots his boots for each shift in December, as if lacing up for combat, as if he'd slay his way through winter for his earnings if he had to. Her leg trembles with anxiety as she sits, back rounded, waiting for his shoe to drop. The man does not waver. She's curious watching him rush to do it all, always leaving their apartment on time at sundown. Just to bring the bacon home.

Each evening, she makes him breakfast for dinner: toast and two eggs, over-easy. Her prescription is kept in a plastic egg tray on the door of the refrigerator in one of the open holes. This is so she remembers. For the couple, Penny's meds are like butter to Cleave's toast—a requirement.

No cracking tonight, she says most nights, then pops the pill, lifts her tongue, and swallows.

After, he hugs her tight, seems to suck her into him the same each night before heading out. When he says, Pen, you're my real live Lucky Penny Girl, she plays along with the routine. Given how Cleave's wife died so young, she tries her best to *feel* for him, for the wife. She tries to understand that it's in Cleave's nature to feel lucky to be alive rather than guilty for surviving. Tragic, really, the whole accident—a young bride taken from her man by a cracked out semi-driver down on old County Road P less than a year after they'd been married. Sometimes, after Cleave leaves, she turns up the radio and sits at the kitchen table thinking of his loss. Just last week, the Beatles' *Yesterday* played right along with the track of her imagining. The song brought a pang to her nose like right before a cry. She closed her eyes, thought harder, even pictured the woman's eyes dulling before she passed. Then, she rolled up her sleeve and pinched herself right under the bicep to cut through the deadening caused by the meds. Pinch for the dead woman's pain and the unspoken agony of her own life. And still, nothing. Love and pain combined didn't even do it for her.

On the meds, life is a wristwatch and she's the broken second hand, wound up but not going anywhere. She's stuck. Numb. Off the meds, life is on fast-forward, one one-thousandth at a time, and every second means something. So, when Cleave hugs her, she exaggerates her embrace to show him she cares, forcing her body to hold onto him just a beat longer than he might expect. She suspects that Cleave's decency comes from his superstition, his belief that how he cares for people makes them die. It's the least she can do then, Penny thinks, to massage his fears about love, to soothe his frail heart with some affection. It's the least she can do given how little it must seem that she really cares about anything. Or anyone, at all.

Oh yeah? Where'd you find me then? she answers, always.

Under that old marquee overhang at Third and Wisconsin where I up and kissed your pretty Penny head for the very first time, he says.

Spun around and there I was, all bright and shiny, I know, I know, Cleave.

Penny can't wrap her mind around it, how his love seems to shield her like an umbrella, certain to follow so long as she doesn't let go. Same treatment each evening he takes off; same when he lands in bed with her later. She wonders if he had the energy to love his wife like this all the way up until she died. Her head rests against the flannel of Cleave's meaty shoulder when she pats him on the behind like he's her dog. For Penny, skepticism is an automatic reaction to Cleave. Her adult conclusions have proven that when it comes to love, suspicion must be fastened, like a seatbelt. It's a safety issue. Doubt is involuntary, like a tic.

After he leaves, Penny listens for Cleave's key in the door. He never forgets to lock her in. She watches him from the kitchen window. His truck reverses while she keeps two fingers on the kitchen light switch. Steady. She waits until he's gone, completely out of sight. LIGHTS ON. LIGHTS OFF. One, two, three times—exactly. Outside, Christmas lights flicker. She thinks they're timed perfectly to her ritual. Penny grins. She takes a deep breath from her gut that makes her feel alive.

LIGHTS ON. *Midwestern winter dawn. Cleave's still gone. Penny knows that cheap wine can keep her going—then bring her down— if she can just hold on.* LIGHTS OFF.

The previous evening, before he headed off, Cleave already smelled like Slim Jims and gasoline. She remembers the scent, and how he'd said, It's Christmastime, baby. Wrap yourself up for me, with jerky and beer on his breath. He unwrapped a piece of Wrigley's Doublemint.

When are you going to let me marry you? he'd said and popped the gum in his mouth. Then, he rolled up the wrapper, twisting the ends together into a ring. Before he got to one knee, he already had her hand in his, trying to mold the aluminum trash around her ring finger.

I mean it, Pen. It's time.

You cannot be serious, Cleave.

Serious as a heart attack.

I will do worse than die on you, she thought.

Let's get hitched, he said.

It's only a matter of time, she thought, until I undo you, too.

LIGHTS ON. *Christmas. Penny was seven when she locked herself behind the bathroom door hiding from her mother. Her tiny body burrowed into the frame of the bathtub. Feeble by dawn, she waited through the entire night—patient and awake—until her mother's psychosis was over. Silent morning. Calm. Her mother flipped a coin after making amends. Heads or tails, Little Girl? Penny never understood how to choose or which side meant she'd won. Heads, Mommy. Wrong. She hated herself for losing the toss. Dry your eyes, my Little Girl, no more crying, Mommy was saved last night, her mother said. Look, Girl, look! The woman's eyes flitted when she opened a hand toward the Girl, a small pool of blood scabbing in a pocket on her palm. Then, she laid her palm across the crown of the Girl's head. The Evil will come for you one day, she said, so you must always be a good Girl, and find*

someone—anyone—who can save you. Her mother licked her finger then, to rub drying blood from the Girl's face. There, she said, all clean, there, there. Two weeks after her eighth birthday, her mother was gone.
LIGHTS OFF.

After his proposal, Cleave stood up to pull her into him. She knew he wanted her to settle down with him—make babies, get a cat. But *this* ... she'd assumed he was done with marriage given his wife's accident. It's what kept her feeling safe in the relationship—clear of any obligation to get better. She'd wondered about her mother then, while against Cleave's chest. One Christmas, years ago, she received a phone call. She caught a shred of breath from across the line. Mother? she'd asked, her longing wedged into the silence just ahead of the dial tone. As if Penny's voice, her recognition, would change her mother's mind. The caller hung up before saying anything. Months went by before she stopped waiting for another call, another try.

He looked as if he would cry when Penny didn't answer him right there, on the spot. Penny knows where the Evil of mania leads; her mother took her there, then left them. In a home where marriages were massacred by mental illness. Where doors slammed shut, winded by wails of loss. Where the survivors—daughter, father—were separated by walls of grief that their cries could never level. So they lived there—in their slaughterhouse—together, caged off from one another, whimpering and wounded.

Penny took the ring from her finger, balled the wrapper into a wad. From fifteen feet away, she shot the ball straight into the kitchen trash bin. Then, she shot him with her big brown eyes. Penny had her mother's eyes. She'd left him standing there alone until she heard the apartment door shut from the bedroom, certain he was gone.

LIGHTS ON. *Now. Kitchen. Trash is on the table. Stacked. Evil's come. At the bottom of the empty plastic trash bin, one prescription bottle. Full. Lithium Carbonate - 600 mg - three times a day - may cause drowsiness. Full! Fuckfuckfuck. Evil be gone.* LIGHTS OFF.

For her father, trying to help his wife was like being outdoors during a tornado. He went underground too late, after she'd already blown through him. In mourning, he sheltered himself from the world, from his daughter. Until eventually, sometime after the mother was gone, the father finally surfaced. He moved on.

When he married Miss Newmother, they both assured the Girl they loved her when she stood beside them in the church as they said their vows after she tossed white petals from a wicker basket at the feet of the guests down the aisle. I love you like my own, Newmother said, as the Girl tugged at the white lace collar of her dress. She remembers being afraid of choking to death, strapped into the bodice of a dress Newmother had chosen, meant for a younger flatter chest. Her son, the Newbrother, said he loved her when, later that very day, he locked her in the guest bathroom during the small reception at their family home and licked the length of her face, from her chin, along her lips, and on up to her forehead. You're so beautiful, he'd said. Our love will be our secret. No one— *not a soul*—can know. I don't want to share you with anyone. For a while, Penny thought how Newbrother touched her was love. At thirteen, she certainly felt old enough to fall in love. She thought the quake in her core—the deep ache that rattled through her like a serpent's tail—was love. Finally, Penny thought, she got it. The love thing.

LIGHTS ON. *Drink. Meds? No pill. Penny wants to feel. No pill, just drink.* LIGHTS OFF.

Then one day, Newbrother enticed the Girl with promises of

a secret present he had for her hidden in the cellar. He took the Girl by the hand as if leading a blindfolded lover to bed—quietly, with real care. In the basement deeps, he shoved himself onto the Girl, her backside pinned against her father's tool rack. When he leaned into her with his mouth on her face, she only remembers cold metal against her spine and a cardboard box beyond the boy labeled as her mother's old belongings. As Newbrother licked and moaned— I *love* you, Girl, he said—she traced the letters on the box with her mind—*KITCHEN DISHES*—and imagined her mother's fragile fingers writing the words.

Newmother dropped her laundry basket when she found them together. Newbrother hit the ground, then curled like a hedgehog at the Girl's feet. The woman spit when she screamed at the Girl standing with her arm across her chest, shirt ripped at the collar, hanging off her shoulders. Girl glanced at Newbrother on the floor, hiding his face with his arms. Strange, she remembers now, how, fetal on concrete in the face of fear, he looked ready for birth, while she stood rigid, positioned for a casket.

She kissed *me*, Mom! She held me down. She made me do it, he said through his tears. The Girl was silent, breathless. Newmother went to her son, crouched down to him to gently guide him upright. She wrapped her arms around him from behind, turning him away from the Girl as if to shield him. It's okay, son, she said. It's okay. When they reached the basement stairs to go up, she turned her head over her shoulder toward the Girl. With her neck bent, she said, I will keep you safe, while her stressed face twisted into knots. She reared like a tiger guarding her cub. For a moment, Penny thought she heard her mother's voice from the mouth of the tiger, that those words were meant for her. Until they left her standing there alone, shuddering.

LIGHTS ON. *Kitchen. Penny's manic, exalted, in worship, on her knees, to really get in there—GET IN THERE, GIRL! she yells in reverence of a high like this. Starting gun. Like a racehorse— whipped—she's off and rushing. Toothbrush to baseboards. Faster. Go.* LIGHTS OFF.

After that, Newbrother broke things off. He stopped touching her. He stopped loving her. When she asked him what was wrong, why he didn't want her, he explained that she just wasn't doing it for him anymore. I have a girlfriend now, Penny, he said. A *real* girlfriend. I can't get caught again with a kid like you. It would ruin everything for me.

But I thought you loved me, Penny said.

Love? he laughed. I can't *court* you, Girl. I never loved you. Not like that, anyhow.

Penny was sick with heartache. She retreated to her bedroom for days, refused to go to school. Arguments began between New-mother and her father, fierce arguments when kitchen knives were hurled like spears, plates broken, thrown like stones. She heard them from the cave of her bed. What should they do with her? What's wrong with her? She needs serious help, and then, Unless you figure this out, Newmother yelled, I will take my son and leave this jungle of a home. You get her fixed or it's over.

The Girl was diagnosed by Doctor Newhope, the same psychiatrist who had treated her mother. She only knew because she remembered the day her mother left, how her father had scurried for the doctor's card with his emergency contact information held behind a magnet on the fridge. Her father explained the reason for their visit, what had led him to bring his daughter in. The Girl blushed sitting in an oversized chair across from the doctor while her father sat beside her, explaining the recent events with Newbrother. She's been erratic, Doctor, impulsive, moody. She seems totally unmotivated one day and enraged, overly excited, the next. Sometimes she won't get out of bed for days, he rambled on, as if listing symptoms of the flu or a common cold. Dr. Newhope wrote the lithium prescription swiftly, pen to paper like a gavel to the bench. He said he was certain this was just what she needed, that the Girl reminded him of her mother. Bipolar. Type 1. Be careful with this one, the doctor told her father on that first visit. If I remember correctly, your wife's behavior escalated quickly. The apple doesn't fall far from the tree, I'm afraid.

The Girl got better. She stabilized. Her father's marriage didn't. I just don't trust her, Newmother said. She's still reckless, and I'm afraid of her becoming undone. I can't subject my son to this. When Newmother and her son pulled away from the curb in their U-Haul, the woman cried. Her father cried. They said they loved each other, that it was all for the best, that they'd stay in touch and take good care, all as the Girl stood some feet away from the huddle, dazed and listless. She did not cry. She did not feel, not even a heartbeat, until Newbrother gave her one last glance from the passenger seat. Through the window, he waved, then mouthed, I will miss you, with a quick wink at the end. Only then did her blood move when her dense heart sank to her toes like a bowling ball. Not sadness, no, *anger*. At just how terrible she was at love. Her eyes averted before his. She felt like the one bad grape at the bottom of the bag, the wilted one that ruins the whole sweet bunch.

When the Girl followed her father back into the empty house that day, she thought she heard him say, You're just like her—your mother. And then, You're doomed. His voice was all too hushed though, all too under-his-breath, to be certain. But the Girl didn't need to ask for a clearer version. She had a deep sense of these wrecked things about herself.

Now, she has that same Little Girl sense, but vaster. A less naive knowing that's unfurled slowly, over time, from a crack into a cavern. Looming madness resides in that hole. Her own insanity. LIGHTS ON. *Three empty cans Heinz baked beans. With bacon! With bacon. One, two, three. Stacked. Eighteen skinny rubber bands. Three: brittle, broken. Two: soft, blue. Stacked. One coffee-stained receipt from Otto's on the East Side for six bottles of chardonnay at a discount. Flattened, drying. Two books of matches. Three matches missing. Stacked.* LIGHTS OFF.

Penny steps back from her heap of arbitrary things. Hands to hips, she looks over the house of cards with a bird's-eye view. Then, she rinses her hands, scrubs each cuticle with a Brillo pad, brand new, right from the box. She bleeds. She rinses. There, all clean, she says, there, there.

LIGHTS ON.

Evil be gone. Gone!

Sixteen Tupperware. Stacked.

Fifteen lids. Stacked.

LIGHTS OFF.

LIGHTS ON. An empty wine bottle hangs off her hand at the end of one limp arm. The other arm hugs her chest like a life vest. She's barefoot, naked from the waist down. Mid-room, she stomps to beats scratched on vinyl in her racing turntable mind. LIGHTS OFF. LIGHTS ON. *She feels for her face as if reading blind, a touch along the foreign words of each socket. Her eyes are like a deer's to light, wide and afraid. H-E-L-P, she mouths. There's no feeling in her bottom half. Nothing at all. She touches her body parts, pats along the length of each bare thigh like a nurse inspects a newborn. Harder now, to feel something—SLAP—to get the child breathing, make her cry. Cry, child, cry! she yells. Then, she does. She cries.* LIGHTS OFF. LIGHTS ON. Then there's nothing. No sound at all. Except her pulse—bolting up her spine, along her nape, lodged into each temple like a bullet. She unscrews another bottle. She sips at first, to settle the hairs at salute on her neck, then throws it all back down her throat. That last one does it for her. She skids into the globe of her body like a parachute landing. A rugged awakening. LIGHTS OFF.

Lights are on. The shrine of items she's arranged reminds her of divinity, the perfect symmetry of small, insignificant things. The way each one is set against the other *means* something. This all has meaning. Doesn't it? Penny shakes her head. It must. It *must*. White morning light splits through a broken slat in plastic blinds covering the kitchen-sink window. Then, she sees their photo, the only one of the couple—Penny and Cleave—together in the same shot. Cleave had the photo framed, said he loved it that much, then propped the frame against the kitchen window on the sill. He said he liked how the light hit their faces from that angle. Like the real thing, the light on the river back then, Pen. Remember? She remembers. Sundown on the Rock River close to when they'd first met, before he knew too much about her. He had a can of Miller in-hand, his arm wrapped around her, and he was smiling. He's always smiling. Penny still had sunglasses on, even at dusk, her head turned down and slightly away from him, from the camera. From the start, she knew she didn't deserve him. His consistency didn't change that, didn't make her feel any different about herself. Looking back, her life had always felt like walking the plank. And now, she'd been bound at the ankles by his proposal. No, she didn't feel safer ... or the least bit secure. She knew she'd disappoint him—one day, down the line. Off the edge, she'd sink them both. LIGHTS OFF.

Down. Come on down. Penny pours her wine into a tall kitchen glass. Down. Hands to knees, she squats before the table in a helmet of matted hair, like a soggy lineman. Penny takes Cleave's frame into her hands. She removes the photo from the glass, then smooths it straight against the table at the head of her littered altar. One of her hands chokes the neck of a wine bottle while the other arm reaches for redemption in her prescription. She closes her eyes, tries to imagine herself in a different photo—white dress, veil pulled back from her face, smiling. She searches the darkness behind her lids for any light, any light at all left in her own wide brown eyes. They'd be looking ahead—the man, yes, and the bride's eyes, too—looking forward, eager to be captured. Where are those eyes? she says. Where are you? And then, She's there, in the darkness. She's here, in the light. She's everywhere. Her mother. Penny opens her eyes. Not in this house, Mother. Not here, she says. This man is too good for saving me.

She drops the pill bottle. Grabs the frame. Glass. Hard. Table. Harder. Edge. Shatter. Its crash unbinds her like key to cage. She's been released. Shards fall to the ground around her bare feet. With the sharpest piece, she etches a line down the center of the photo, separating herself from Cleave. Then, she continues, from the photo's corner, through the middle of her face, her neck, her chest. She scratches at the photo until the glass pierces through exactly where her heart would be. Suddenly then, she's crying … she's wailing … stop. She's laughing … STOP. Her hand. She's bleeding. Right in the center of her palm. All at once, she's calm.

She balls her fist, squeezes tight, then creases the photo down its center. Cleave is placed face up with shreds of her likeness on paper folded back, behind him. Then, with a broad sweep of her arm, she dumps the other tabled items into an empty bag. All the trash she's come to adore … means *nothing*, nothing. She ties the bag quickly. Tighter. Blood runs down the white plastic bag as she carries it to the door. Get it gone, all of it, *gone*. She wants all that Evil—her mother, herself—out of the house. Be gone. Morning has come. Cleave will be home from the graveyard shift soon. She slides into her slippers to drag the bag to the dumpster outside.

Open air. She breathes. Frozen air like waste from her lungs. She sets the bag down on snow. Look, Girl, look. She sees. Flat endless Midwestern gray miles. Naked branches of maple trees snag the horizon—sharp—like needles to cloth. A bassinet of gray webbed between cushy blue spruce where, she thinks, spiders can rest. She wraps her arms around herself. It's all so … destitute. And beautiful. Could she be like this, a beautiful gray mess?

Beyond the alley, a family builds a snowman. A family—man, woman, child. The man holds the boy high in his arms to cap the snowman while the woman ties a scarf around its neck. They stand aside, arms locked, to see what they've made—all three, together. The boy runs off then, to the nearest maple, snaps twigs off the ends of branches. He hurries back, slides to a crouch. Knees to snow, he constructs the snowman's fingers, its toes. Delicate, she can see, the boy's touch—the way he treats his sculpture, taking his time to make it right. Penny's mother had tended to her at times like that, before she left, when things were decent, sane. Mother on meds made the whole world feel safer, more contained. Those times they'd played together—mother and daughter—in the snow, angels and ice skates on the pond behind her childhood home. I can't believe these trees, her mother said. They were just saplings when we moved here. They're beautiful full-grown maples now. They'd made a snowman that day, too, with pennies for eyes—one eye: heads, the other: tails. She'd been given both sides of her mother all in one that day—a whole complete woman. A real mother, who was careful, cautious, as if her world was made of eggshells, and Penny, her precious yolk. Penny remembers she could breathe back then, when her mother's tread was light and soft. Breathe. Just like this. There *were* good days, weren't there? There were. She looks to the family in the distance. They seem so *alive*, golden against the gray. Penny even sees life in the man they made out of snow.

Penny lifts the trash bag. She thinks then—when bagged bottles hit metal—that she's finally got it covered. She wipes her hands together. She's done. She'll go back, back home, to Cleave, to clean up her mess, make things right, take her meds. She will. She can choose. Can't she? Her mother chose. She *will*. She would have. But then, then, there he is.

The Stranger. He comes from the backside of the dumpster when its lid hits the lip. You must be cold, he says, eyes up, down, all over her. Madonna tour T-shirt down to her knees. Bunny slippers, gray ears dragged through snow. Dried blood on her hand from palm to tips. His eyes are wide, brown, wanting. Dark bags under each have slumped close to his cheek line. A lit cigarette hangs from his mouth, and he's got a can of Miller in his hand. He looks as though he's been awake for days.

You lost? he asks.

No, she says. You?

I live right over there. He points down the alley.

Me too. She points the other direction. What time is it?

Morning, I bet. You want a drink?

No, she says. I don't even know who the fuck you are. Nope. No way.

You sure? He hands the can toward her.

Those eyes. As if begging for something to hide. The Stranger's eyes remind her of her mother's hollow eyes. Of her own. Penny stares at him. Frozen.

Well? The Stranger shakes the can toward her.

Blink. Familiar calm, a sterile soft spot. The moment right before a storm a dog might sense. When there's space to consider what damage might get done. But the sensing does not stop the storm from coming. It's inevitable. Like loving Newbrother. Unavoidable. Like a father's fear of his daughter. Fixed. Like a little plastic wind-up toy, a jumping monkey that falls flat on its face. Predictable. Isn't it? Always has been. Blink.

Take it, he says. You know you want to.

She tilts her head then, to change her view of him. A younger Stranger would have reminded her of Newbrother with that longing in his eyes. Back then, she was tethered to him, in tow simply because he said so. Back then, she would have allowed this man to overcome her. She digs her slippered heels into the snow. No longer. Her whole life she's been bridled by her illness. Leashed and dragged. Her mother took control when she left. No meds, no family to restrain her. Penny wants to feel reins like those in her own two hands. This time, there will be no flip of the coin, no. No surrender to the mechanics of meds or the fate of a mother's choice, a brother's demands. She will not give in. Not even to Cleave's appeal. Random infidelity will seal the deal. This time, *she will choose*. Suddenly, Penny understands how to be unfettered. How to taste freedom as if with her mother's tongue.

She takes the can. Downs it all. Tosses the empty into the bin. The Stranger reaches toward her. She takes his hand.

He leads Penny down the alley, the back way to his one-room apartment on the far side of the complex. As she follows him, she looks back toward her own apartment in the other direction. She thinks of Cleave, at home, waiting. Then, she looks for the family from before, in the distance—mother, father, son. They must've gone. The snowman's still there. His head's melting now, slumped into his body, and one of his eyes has fallen out. Things are falling apart. She leaves her grayed bunny slippers at the Stranger's door after he closes it behind her. Locked.

LIGHTS ON. The Stranger pours red wine from a box into a mug for her. He pours his into an old Slurpee cup, sucks on a straw. She drinks it all. Her bare legs are numb, red, raw. She steps to the middle of the room. He sets his cup down. Let me look at you, he says. He removes the wool scarf from around his neck, holds it taut by each end. Then, he circles her in slow steps. She feels wrangled, like a wild horse. He moves around her front, to her side. Then, he stops at her back. His heat chills her even more. Her shoulders round when he wraps the scarf around her, folding her into the thing. They sway together like that, strapped in—high—as if at the door of a plane, ready to jump. She closes her eyes. No fear. LIGHTS OFF.

She's on his bed. On her back. Face up. He's coming closer, each piece of clothing left on the floor behind him like a snake sheds its skin. Then, his body is across hers, her T-shirt still between them. She's surprised by how slow he moves, how much time he takes to loosen her. There's a window beyond him. One window. Look, Girl, look. Look at the sky. One slice of blue cuts through gray. When the blue bleeds through, she *feels* something. Keep going, she says to the Stranger. Just do it, she says. You're going too slow. But that light, that bloody blue, bright and spreading … she's caving … not into him, no—she's opening into what she sees beyond this room, what could come to be.

She sees herself later, older, seaside, surrounded by blue. She'll be reminded of the Stranger then by the blueness of a massive summer sky. She'll shade her eyes and lounge. Head tilted back, she'll peruse the memory of the intimate wrangling as if tiptoeing through forbidden rooms. She'll lose herself in the blueness as if diving for treasure. She'll find her recollection shipwrecked, corroding in the deeps of the basement blues, half-eaten with little rusty bits floating to the surface. Bits of how the Stranger's moans were brazen like trumpets, and the mattress was bare with a heart-shaped stain, and how she noticed the warped tune of a distant ice-cream truck when he came, and how his inner thigh smelled like baby powder and burnt toast. Bits of Newbrother's cellar and cement, of a mother's heads and tails, of a father's misery and moderation. She'll weave her fingers into Cleave's with him at her side. Wait, she thinks, there's still time. A gray mess can make me beautiful. *My choice.* I decide.

Stop, she groans at the Stranger, StopStopStop, she yells, STOP! Then, she bolts.

Cleave's sitting in the kitchen when she breaks through. He's still. His back is straight, hands resting on his lap. He's facing the front door, toward her. He'll be off to work for another shift soon. His boots are laced. She tries to speak while he stares at her, drenched in chaos. She can't catch her breath. She scans the room. Breathing. Her wreck has been managed. Cleave must've cleaned it all up. There are Christmas lights hanging along the edge of the kitchen window, and below that, resting on the sill, there's a different photo of the couple. In a new frame. In this one, she can see her eyes.

You're safe, he says. I'm glad.

Something happened today.

I'm sure it did.

We need to talk.

I'm sure we do.

You didn't have to clean up my mess, Cleave.

It's what family does.

You're not my family.

That depends on which side of things you're looking at.

I'm damaged goods, she says.

Me too, he says. I drink. People die.

Chances are, I will do worse than die on you.

I would like to take my own chances, Girl.

He walks toward her then. He wraps his arms around her. She nestles her head into him. Then she says, What if I end up just like her? in sounds muffled by his warm shoulder. He draws himself away from her. He moves his hands to level her shoulders, presses down gently, as if he's planting her, a sapling to ground. You are not your mother, he says.

Penny walks past him to the kitchen table. Her prescription sits beside an empty can filled with water to hold one daffodil, head hanging over, heavy on its stem. Cleave. She opens the bottle. Takes all three. She looks to him. He's smiling when he says, Let's just take our time. We'll take our chances—together. Then, he reaches into his jeans pocket. You call it, Pen. He opens his hand. Heads or tails? When he tosses the penny high, she sees the aluminum ring balled up beside the pill bottle. Well, what's it going to be? he says, while Penny wonders what the chances are of the coin landing on its edge.

FISH AND FLOWERS

OUTSIDE WAITING. JOAN hates waiting, hates standing still. She's outside in the passenger pickup area right where she said she'd be. Tailwinds pushed her connection into Seattle from Chicago ahead of schedule. She bypassed baggage claim with one bag over her shoulder. In the backpack, a balled-up black dress, black spiked heels, a stained cosmetics bag with dried out mascara and red lipstick, a curling iron with a frayed cord. Items she had to dig for. Three empty airplane bottles of whiskey roll around somewhere near the bottom. She checks her watch. Joan hates this, being held up. She's waiting for a ride from her younger sister. Maureen is like a mosquito bite she can't help but scratch. Irritation is a given.

She's got a double espresso from Starbucks in one hand. Black, no sugar. She drinks. A lit cigarette in the other. Drags. Checks her watch. Waits. One lady hurries by like Joan's got the plague, waving her hand to clear the smoke, other hand cupped over her nose. She coughs when she passes. One loud intentional hack and a glare. That's how Joan knows how things have changed. Apparently, you can't smoke *anywhere* in Seattle now, not even in open public spaces. It's been so long since she's been back to her hometown, Joan's got no idea about the change in social mores. She snuffs out the smoke then flicks the butt on the ground, near the woman's feet. This place reeks of pretense. Joan can actually smell bullshit in the air, a fishy tang hanging on the mist off the Sound. Fancy people in trendy clothes carrying small, jacketed dogs bred to fit in baskets. The whole thing stinks.

Where is she? Come on, Maureen. Christ. She pulls the collar of her leather jacket up around her ears, crosses her arms at her chest. She lights another cigarette, blows the first drag toward one airport security guard who seems to have his eye on her. He taps on a posted sign behind him, *NO SMOKING WITHIN 25 FEET OF BUILDING ENTRANCE*. She holds her hands up as if being arrested. Freeze! She yells, You got me, officer, and takes a few slow, deliberate steps backward toward the street. Then, she rolls her eyes and turns forward. She looks down the road for her ride.

Joan hates her sister more than she hates the waiting. Hates her. In the same unreasoning way she imagines other people hating Mexicans or Indians, with real gusto and tenacity. She imagines her baby sister like one of those Barbie dolls that smile relentlessly but can only move their limbs at the joints. Flawless waistline but with absolutely no distinguishing marks of character. She's always wanted to pop the head right off that doll. Oh, but her mother, her mother just *adored* the girl. Naturally, one of them would be loved more than the other, given their threesome, how Ma had raised them on her own. Sure as Seattle rain, Joan knows that Mo's the favorite. Seemed to her Ma had been elated, almost relieved, when Joan had run all the way to the other side of the country, leaving her all freed up to nest with Maureen, the perfect Disney princess. It was a deliberate move, miles placed like dominoes between them, the stockpile of time.

She wonders how long this will all take, how long she'll have to

be here to show her due respect. Is there a standard? An appropri-
ate amount of time meant for burying your dead mother? Joan's got
no protocol for death. She's managed quite well to avoid her family,
to dodge anyone's dying. Maureen's as good as dead to her, sure, but
she's still living. Joan straightens her back, stretches her neck. She's
here for good reason, damn it. She's made a solid choice. Right?
She smokes. Despite distance, the link to her mother remains fastened, heavy across her shoulders like a yoke. Now, she's come for
the unburdening. Ma is the one tent stake in a windstorm, anchor-
ing a tiny sliver of her to Seattle. If nothing else, she's here for the
sacrament of cutting any final ties that bind her to this place. Yes,
the right choice. Good thing she packed light. Rest assured, she'll
be on the next flight back to the East Coast the second Ma's funeral
is over. After this, she'll never have to come back.

Joan checks her watch again. Twenty-eight minutes late. She
spits old gum and menthol toward the street, then props her backpack against a bench. She hates how clean everything is around
here, like it's all been staged. That's the problem she sees. And these
people? Joan watches as a woman embraces her man at the car
curbside when he arrives to pick her up. The way she kisses him,
one peck on each cheek, like even their affection has been rehearsed.
Boring. She likes things raw. Her East Coast city with all that haze
and exhaust, old lotto tickets and cigarette butts floating in rain
puddles rushing toward sewer drains, city grime reminding her of
the million other lives beyond her own. She already misses her real
home, her small sixth-floor apartment where she can pour herself
a tall whiskey, on the rocks of course. She'd stir the drink with her
finger and drop an ice cube from the glass into the shriveling cactus,
half-dead on a window ledge overlooking the alley behind the
building. The view makes her feel safe, like she's underground, with

all the other mistakes and rats of the world, where she can ad-lib her days. Pick any hour in the city, and you can get lost in people's impromptu lives. Her city is where she can hide. No, this place hasn't been home since she left at seventeen.

Fuck this. She tosses her cigarette on the ground, digs for her phone to call a cab. Just as she's about to dial, there she is, Maureen. Her sister rolls the passenger window down. Joan leans in, sticks her head through.

Late much? Joan says, elbows propped on the window's edge.

We said quarter after.

Yeah, and it's quarter till.

Thirty minutes, Joan. Is it really the end of the world?

Joan tosses her backpack through the open window toward the back seats and gets in. It's been a long time, little sis. How you been?

Ma died, Joan. It's been a lot to handle.

You always knew how to handle everything. I'm sure you did fine.

They're still idling when Maureen reaches into her purse. She comes back with a manila envelope that she tosses into Joan's lap. I just came from the attorney's office, Joan. That's why I was late. We were reviewing Ma's will.

Joan sets the envelope on the dash. She unlaces her boots and pulls her feet out. Then, she rests her socked feet on top of the envelope and takes a cigarette from her pack to tuck behind her ear. She leans back, arms behind her head, then looks to her sister.

A will. She had a will?

She did. It's right there. Maureen points to the envelope.

What for? The house will go to you. And what else has she got to give away?

Well, that's the thing, Joan.

What's the thing, Maureen? Behind them a car honks. Maureen looks ahead, lips pursed. Joan flips them off through the window. Go around us, assholes! she yells. Well, what is it? Joan says to her sister.

I don't know how to say this.

Jesus, what's with all the drama? Joan takes the cigarette from her ear and balances it between her lips. She leans forward. Just say it, Mo. Spit it out.

Maureen begins pulling out from the curb. Then, with her eyes in the rearview mirror, she says, Well, Joan, it seems as though Ma, she ... she left the house to *you*.

They're already on the road when Joan snatches the envelope from the dash. What the fuck? She rips open the envelope to take the papers out, flipping pages until the end. Then, she stops. She looks at Maureen. Joan notices wrinkles around her eyes, that her mouth is drawn down. She sees gravity in the lines of her little sister's face. Maureen tucks her hair behind her ears and looks to Joan. The only color Joan sees in her skin is at the tips of Maureen's ears, fiery along the edges.

Holy shit, Maureen. I don't ...

She left you a note, also. It's in there somewhere.

Joan shakes the empty envelope and onto her lap falls a single piece of paper. Joan closes her eyes and takes a breath. Then she lays the paper on her lap, smoothing Ma's handwriting against her thighs. *Use this home for a safe place to be ... If you need help taking care of the house, ask your sister ...* Joan runs her finger across the lines *... Just come home, Joanie ... I forgive you for leaving ... I'm sorry I never thanked you ...* then, at the very end *... I love you, I do ... I love you BOTH.* Joan slaps her hands down. She stuffs the papers back into the envelope, throws it back on the dash like she's been burned.

This cannot be right, Joan says.

Apparently, she wants you more ... *involved.*

What are we going to do?

The question seems to be, what are *you* going to do, Joan.

It's just, I just ... I don't get it. I've been gone for a lifetime.

I think that's the point, Joan.

I don't understand.

That makes two of us, for once.

You should get the house. No question. You stayed around.

Well, imagine that. After all this time, here we are, agreeing on something. Maureen reaches over to Joan. She grabs the cigarette right from her mouth. Give me a light, she says. Then she rolls down her window. Mist wets her face while she lights the cigarette. Maureen holds the thing way out the window with a French manicure and a diamond the size of Texas. Joan has never seen her little sister smoke. She looks completely out of her element, like some soccer mom in a strip club.

Ho-ly shit, Ma, Joan whispers. Suddenly, she feels an ache in her throat. She pinches the bridge of her nose, closes her watery eyes. She keeps her gaze out the window, mouth shut, while Maureen smokes down to the filter and drives them home.

Beacon Hill. The sisters arrive without saying another word. Maureen parks in the driveway. She gets out fast, as if trying to escape. Joan takes her time. She closes the car door. Rests herself against the car. Lights a cigarette. She needs to think.

In front of her, there's the house she'd left behind so many years ago. Maureen's already inside. She's surprised how outdated the bungalow looks, like a sore thumb on the Hill with its blistering periwinkle paint and crooked front porch. But its dilapidation fits perfectly against that sweet-and-sour view of Seattle with Mt. Rainier protruding like a perfect porcelain crowned tooth. She drags hard on her cigarette, exhales toward the neighboring houses crouched in with angled stoops, fenced in by unkempt gardens of creeping mosses and untamed flowers—yellow black-eyed Susans, pink tulips, lavender morning glories, red bleeding hearts. Then, she thinks she sees her mother there. In her own garden. She's crouched but turned toward Joan. Joan can't quite make out her face under the wide brim of a wicker hat. Her eyes are shaded. She's got those thick gardening gloves on. Same pair she wore all those years. Same as always back then.

Come to the garden, Joanie. You can help me plant my roses. Grab my gloves on your way out. A young girl, she'd slide her small hands into the worn leather gloves, fingers baggy at the ends. She was closest to her mother then, imagining her hands like little seeds sprouting under the shelter of Ma's leather. A basket sits beside her for lilies she'd clip. Ma cuts the flowers special for dinner on Sundays. Fish from Pike Place Market. Same as always. The flowers are set in the middle of the table in a blue vase.

Yellow dust stains your nose when you get too close, and then you're left with sweetness in your nostrils all night. You help her do the dishes on Sundays. Like a good girl. You love to help her. She washes, you dry. You're careful with the blue vase. *Make sure you dry it, Joanie. Careful. No streaks.* You work hard to wipe each smudge. Then, held only by its rim, you stretch the vase toward her, proud and smiling. One time, when she reaches down toward you for the blue vase, your wet hands lose their grip. The vase slips. Ma swoops in to catch the heirloom inches from the floor. *I told you to be careful. How many times do I have to say it? Clumsy girl.* She turns away, sends you out of the room. Next time in the garden, when Ma yanks her big leather gloves off your small hands, you will remember how she turned away from you when you failed her. You will remember how she replaced you with Maureen to help with dinner. How relieved Ma seemed when Maureen took over. You promise yourself to try harder. The gloves are folded—each finger arranged with care—then set back in place where your mother will see them. During the weeks of childhood, the empty blue vase is stored on top of the refrigerator until next Sunday for fish dinner. Same as always.

Joan looks up. Jesus, Ma. What am I supposed to do here? She takes the walkway through the front garden up to the house. Bloated gray skies hush the neighborhood on her wary walk to the front door. Not even a bark to be heard. Joan remembers young families back in the day—kids on bikes, bats on balls, everything in motion. She takes a drag, flips her collar, and rounds her shoulders into a cage. She's at the porch when the sun cocks back and fires the first round of light through a dense cloud.

She sets a boot on the first step of the depressed porch. A spider nests in the top corner of the porch overhang. She sees how the light glimmers and reflects off its web and follows the thread to its end point, down low, where she used to sit in the shade. Where was that spot? Where she'd land in shadows, sneaking smokes against the high, wide view. The mountain's assault of ice and light ricochets off the house. She squints, pulls her shades down, all in black, fluttering like an insomniac bat in daylight. She imagines herself falling through the foundation of this house like quicksand, then being sucked under right along with the old home and all the old things they shared, strangled by all those damn flowers gone rampant. Joan crouches, runs her hand under the lip of the top stair.

Crawling her fingers around, she finds it right away—the big nub of wadded gum she'd saved up all those years. It feels permanent as a handprint in cement.

You left here, this home, at seventeen. From this very stoop. Nights before, your little sister was at your bedroom door when she was supposed to be sleeping. It was late. Your boyfriend clipped the bedroom window with a pebble to tell you to let him in. Let me in, Joan, hurry. Slinking through, he hands off a bottle of booze. To share. You're drunk when he climbs on top. He pulls the covers above your heads. His knees are on either side of your ribcage. Then, he kneels on your arms. The skin is pinched, tacked to the bed by his shins. He leans into your face. Breathes hot into your ear, deep like a foghorn. His mouth is wet. Then, your face is hot and wet from his mouth. He seems to pant like an animal. You've never done this before. Shh, you say, be quiet. My sister's room is right next door. He moves both hands down to your hips. His face is smashed into the pillow beside yours. He moves at the waist. Stop making so much noise, you say, because he's grunting, he's groaning. Your eyes are scrunched closed when he props his torso upright to throw the covers back. He kneads your breasts like dough, tugging and twisting. It hurts. It all hurts. Finally, he stops moving. He slumps himself off to your side. You open your eyes, gaze toward the door for comfort, for the feeling of leaving here. And there she is, her one eye. Your little sister through the crack in the open bedroom door. You cry only once during the whole painful thing. When, after locking eyes with Maureen, you hear her footprints skitter like a tiny mole on the floor outside your door.

The following evening. Sunday dinner. You're hungover in your bedroom. Door shut. You lie face down on the bed. Your abdomen is sore, and your arms are bruised from where he kneeled on your body to pin you down. You yank your sleeves down to your wrists. A Walkman blasts Black Sabbath in your ears. The noise helps drown out the shame screeching in your head like mating cats. Maureen and Ma are in the kitchen working together on dinner. You move one headphone to the side of your ear to listen.

Maureen's sobbing in the kitchen. You roll your eyes. When Maureen was a baby, chicken pox ravaged her body. *Run and get me the lotion, Joan. Quickly! Can't you see your sister's in pain?* You stand aside at the bathroom door while your mother draws a bath. *Oatmeal, Joan. Run!* Maureen's agony brings tears of suffering to your mother's own eyes. You return with the canister of oats and a spoon. *Ground oatmeal. Not that one!* Back to the kitchen, you scurry, scramble, sprint. Finally, you get it right. You scoop the powder—steady, now, steady—balance the spoon. Tiptoe toward Ma at the side of the tub. *Give me that, Joan. I don't need another mess.* She snaps the canister from the crook of your arm to dump the oatmeal in. Then you remember Ma's herb garden, what she'd taught you when you were allowed to help her, that chamomile calms the skin. Quickly, you grab scissors from the drawer, dart to the garden. You rifle for the herb—that's the one! pluck, snip—then back to the tub, hands extended with the little yellow flowers wilting in your sweaty palm. *What's this? DANDELIONS? In heaven's name. Leave us, Joan, just go.* Maureen, moaning. Ma cradling Maureen in her arms to lift her from the tub—holding, soothing, rocking, smoothing, kissing your sister's pockmarked skin. Milky warm water softens her scabs. Ma pats her daughter dry, then dots each blister with calamine while the girl wails and wails, her face purple as a grape from the strain. Maybe the kitchen needs cleaning. You leave them there, tending to wounds together, while you try to find your use.

Maureen's been crying for attention ever since, even at sixteen.

When she didn't make the varsity cheerleading team, she cried and got hugs from your mother. Then Ma took her out for ice cream, the two of them, together. When an older girl was chosen for homecoming queen, she cried and got to watch her favorite movie. Ma and Mo cuddled under one blanket, the two of them, together. She cried when she wasn't smart enough for AP, when she failed her first driving test, when she was picked last for the softball team. The more she'd cry the more of Ma she got, the two of them, always together.

Then, there's you, the other one.

You: the older one.

You: the stronger one.

You: the taller, rougher, plainer one.

You: the no-one wo-man of the house where there is no-man.

Ma, look at me, I got an A on my biology test.

Find your sister, Joan. You must watch out for her.

Ma, look at me, I got you these flowers at the market.

Find me different ones, Joan. These are half-dead. They simply will not do.

Ma, look at me, I'm lonely.

Find someone else, Joan. Your sister. I'm busy with your sister.

You: always finding. Never being found.

In your bedroom that evening, when you hear your sister crying in the kitchen, you decide from that moment forward, you'll hate her. You'll find shade—the unfamiliar deeps of the house, the corners no one has use for—where you can hide. From the shadows, you will watch Maureen cry for the love you want. She will capture your mother with her weakness, her cries. The pink and lovely girl—your perfect, weepy, sickly sister. Your hatred for how she manipulates will darken and fester like a lesion.

In the other room, Maureen's wailing drones on and on and on. Finally, you've had it up to here with her, you can't take it anymore. You rip the headphones from your ears, stomp to the kitchen. You're in the doorway. Ma holds Maureen. She sobs, pushing her face into the curve of your mother's chest. Her shoulders lift and tumble with each long sob. Ma has her apron on. Sunday fish in an oven pan on the counter.

What the hell happened? you say.

Ma pulls away from Maureen, takes the girl's face in her hands, then covers her ears. *Look what you've done,* she snaps at you. Then, she removes her hands from your sister's ears. *It's okay, darling,* she says to Maureen, and kisses her forehead.

Me? you ask, eyeing Maureen, then Ma.

You've traumatized your sister.

What did *I* do?

Lips pursed, Ma scrubs the counter with a sponge, shifting the pan of fish from here to there. She adjusts her apron, ties a tight bow in the back. Drawers are flung open, then slammed shut. The way she moves shows how angry she is—short stops like skates to ice. Finally, she stands still. When she slams her hands down, fish quivers on the pan.

You know what you did.

Your gaze darts toward Maureen, trying to capture her eyes. Maureen's wiping her tears with the cuff of her sleeve, then turns her back to you. She leans against the sink, head bent forward, sobbing.

What did she tell you?

She told me the truth, Joan. The truth. Which is clearly beyond your capabilities.

What the fuck? Maureen, look at me, you say.

Your behavior is even filthier than your language, Ma says over Maureen's moans.

Jesus, Mo, stop crying.

Leave her alone, Joan.

What did you tell her?

Maureen keeps her back turned. Then she says, I told her what I *saw* with my own two eyes, Joan. That *thing* of a boy you had in your room last night.

In that moment, you stop breathing completely. Blood rushes to the top of your head like water to a hydrant. You want to strangle her right then and there with your bare hands. You can actually feel her thin neck in your palms, the crack of each tiny bone you snap. You imagine her as the Barbie doll you'll come to know as Maureen, head completely popped off. Good as dead.

Ma, I can explain.

There was a boy in your bed, Joan. What more is there to explain?

We were just talking, Ma.

That's not what your sister thinks.

She doesn't know what she saw, Ma. Please.

I do not want your sister subjected to this.

Well what then? you say. What now?

Your mother walks to the refrigerator. She takes the blue vase in her hands, sets it on the counter. With both hands around its base, she looks at you and says, *You never could quite get things right, Joan. But* this? *Now this is not just wrong, it's an* insult. *To me and your sister.*

What about me, Ma?

What about you?

You: I try to do *good* things.

You: I try to do *helpful* things.

You: I try to do *special* things.

All you care about is *her*. All this time. This is my one mistake. What about all the *right* things I try to do?

You, you, you, Joan. You'd like to talk about you? *Alright,* Ma says. She squeezes the vase. Knuckles turn red. *You: did a vile thing …* she extends the blue vase … *You: did a repugnant thing …* she lifts her arms, a samurai to her sword … *You: are supposed to look out for us.* Then, she screams, *You: are USELESS!* She aims the blue vase at her own feet. When it shatters around her bare ankles, she's still howling. No words. Her face is loose, not crumpled with anguish or fear. No, this sound is deep, hollow, unending, like the wail of heartbreak. Or regret.

Your headphones still hang on your neck, Black Sabbath banging at your breast, when Ma walks toward the broom closet. Each of her steps over shattered glass feels like you are the one biting down. Maureen's sobbing all over again. Harder now. You try to move toward them. To help. I can get that, Ma. Let me clean it up, you say, inching toward the broom closet. But Ma extends her palm toward you—stop—like a guard.

No, she says. *Get out of my sight.* Then, she moves toward your sister with open arms. She holds Maureen's face in her hands like a gem, smooths her hair, then tucks her head into the pouch of her collarbone. *There, there,* Ma says. *I'm sorry, darling, I'm sorry.*

You pivot to walk away when she says, *One more thing, Joan, and listen good.* You stop. Your shoulders hike up to your ears and your mouth flinches like, here comes a left hook. Then, at your back, she says, *As sure as October rain, Joan, you will never … and I mean never, see that boy again. You can count on that.*

Fuck this, is all you can manage to say through the rage. You leave the room imagining Ma on her hands and knees sweeping tiny blue shards from cracks in the linoleum.

You did, though, didn't you? You did see that *thing* of a boy again. The very next night after Ma forbade you. He picked you up in his black Camaro. At midnight, after everyone had gone to bed. You waited on this stoop, here. Then, just like that, you were gone. It's the last you saw of the house. Right here. This very stoop.

Years later, on the other side of the country, you will have gone through many, many angry men. One night, you will cry into the bathroom mirror after one of them leaves you. You'll see your mother's face in your own reflection, a purple welt blooming near your left eye. You miss her so terribly then, your mother. You'll consider calling her to check in. To say you're sorry for leaving in the middle of the night without telling her. To say how weak and scared her stronger girl is. How it feels to need to hide the shame of bruises on your bones and under your eyes.

Instead, when you call, you'll talk about the weather or other meaningless, empty things. From your sixth-floor cityscape apartment, you'll say, I think I'm going to get a plant, Ma, across the line, over thousands of miles, while you poke your finger into the dry dirt of a dying cactus.

Oh yeah? You sure you can handle that, kiddo?

Or maybe I'll hold off for a while.

Hold off for what, dear?

Life, Ma. Until I figure out the meaning of life.

I'm sure you'll figure it all out, dear.

You know she knows. She's experienced with concealed feelings. With the hiding. You can feel her knowing abiding in long spaces between vacant words where you wait for an apology—some kind of recognition—like a criminal gone good. But you're not good, are you? No, you've matured into undeserving like a pup fills out its collar until your throat is choked by guilt, and you simply cannot ask. You will continue to feel each other's pain laced into the vibration of small talk until the last time you speak, late one night. Loose-lipped and propped against the jukebox at the low-lit end of the bar, you'll make the final call from your local corner pub around midnight. You'll take the last swig at the bottom of your glass, pull a cigarette from behind your ear to light. Stumble to a payphone at the back of the bar, next to the restroom.

She sounds slow, tired. You ask her if she's feeling alright.

Yep, just about right, kiddo, except for this little ache in my spine. Must be the rain.

She hangs up first, leaving you with the receiver in-hand, dial tone ringing in your ear. You stare at the mouthpiece with longing, then set it back on the hook. A pit opens in your belly then, a cavern wide enough to sink in. You down another shot before leaving the bar, drowning in the feeling that Ma's end is near.

Joan stretches her legs to stand up on the porch. It's been so long since she's been here, she can't imagine how this house somehow now belongs to her. When she opens the front door, she walks through with dread as if opening an engagement ring box from someone you know—deep down—you don't love. The thought of agreeing to the arrangement turns her stomach like a hundred-foot drop off a ledge. She's actually sickened by the responsibility. Inside, Joan treads lightly like the home is a library. Maureen is sitting in the front room. She sits cross-legged in Ma's old chair, high heels strewn on the floor at the foot. Her feet are bare, and Joan can see her toes barely visible, sticking out beneath each knee. Joan swears she's the kid she remembers, but only from the waist down. The rest of her body is held rigid. Her face looks chiseled like an angry antique doll.

Joan sets her backpack in the corner of the room. She smooths her hair back away from her face and loops it into a low bun at the base of her neck. She sits on the armrest of the couch, legs open to either side. Reaches into her pocket for a cigarette, throws the pack on the table ahead. She looks up at Maureen with the unlit smoke hanging from the corner of her mouth, lighter in hand. I need a drink, she says.

You can't smoke in here, Maureen says, shoving the pack toward Joan from the table. People will want to stop by and give their condolences after the ceremony tomorrow. I don't want this place to stink.

Joan moves to the old liquor cabinet. Rummages to find a full bottle of Jack Daniel's, twists the dusty cap off with the cuff of her sleeve. There are two glasses on top of the cabinet, face down. She thinks of her mother drinking from the glass she pours for her sister. The other she pours heavy, for herself. She sets a glass in front of Maureen.

We're going to have to figure out what to do about all of this, Joan says.

What's there to figure out, Joan? Maureen takes a drink. The house is yours, she says. After all the time I stayed and tried to take care of Ma after you left. Maureen finishes her drink, and sets the glass down, hard. It's yours now. Figure it out. She stands up and grabs her heels. The spikes are like daggers in her hands when she leans toward Joan before spinning around to walk away.

You act as if I asked for this, Joan shouts toward Maureen's back as she ascends the stairs. I don't belong here, she says, resting her head in her hands. I don't deserve this house, Ma, she says to herself. What have you done?

Joan pours herself another drink, taller than the last. Downs it fast. Then, she grabs the bottle by its neck. It hangs from her hand while she roams the home as if being led by some invisible docent through an old museum. She looks up at the curio shelves and tabletops in the hall and there, spread before her, are all the trinkets: Mickey Mouse with his left ear chipped from being dropped down the crease of the back seat in the old station wagon on the trip to Disneyland when you were eight, the miniature metal soldiers, guns drawn, tiny seashells sprinkled at their feet. You and Maureen had collected those together in the rain, stopped at Battle Beach that time on the coastal drive through Oregon. Joan drinks, keeps looking, gets stuck on the small things her mother kept arranged in corners or on ledges or propped against the mantle. Odd that right in the middle is an old deck of cheap tarot cards, precisely placed among the clutter, face up and fanned out. You'd insisted on the fifty cents from Ma to buy these out of an old-timey cigarette machine, at the rest stop along the Pacific Coast Highway. That same family trip. You'd covered Maureen's little hand in yours, over the plastic dispenser peg and, together, yanked hard until the deck was finally released. You played with your sister and those cards in the back seat the whole way down the coast to California and back up. Joan walks to the base of the stairs. Maureen's up there. Suddenly, she wants to be with her sister. With one foot on the first stair, she considers going up, running her fingers along the wooden banister. But then, she startles at what she sees disappear as she swipes—faint fingerprints. Her Ma's prints. Joan steps back from the stairs.

She walks down the hallway. Drinks from the bottle. Orange shag carpet, same as always. Along the wall stretches a row of family photos behind cheap frames, as lopsided now as they were back when. She makes it to her old childhood bedroom, stumbling into the walls like a bumper car off the rails. She touches the doorknob. Turns. On the doorframe, you see where Ma etched your heights in the wood. You learned to puff up in the chest to gain a notch over Maureen, standing tall when Ma smiled down on you. Maureen's nick was always the mark closer to the floor.

Inside, Joan's teenage bed is still made with those hospital corners Ma insisted on. She dumps herself on the bed and lies back, spinning. There were phone calls, weren't there? The times little Maureen would call from across the country to tell you how Ma was getting sadder. She called a lot right after you left. Her young teenage voice, Hi Joanie. It's Maureen, your sister. Um, yeah, we miss you here. Especially Ma. Ma seems to be really upset. Really, really … sad. I mean, she cries a lot. Call me back, okay? Just call me. After a lot of unanswered calls, she got the message and stopped trying.

Joan struggles with the cap of the bottle before taking another swig. Then, she cradles the bottle close to her, rocking it like a newborn. She touches along the curve of her elbow, feels the muscle of it, even now, the skin . . . manly and rough. An old Metallica poster torn at the corners still hangs above the bed now dressed in a crisp, white-lace comforter. She rips the poster down, throws it toward the door when she sees Maureen standing there, watching, like all those years ago. This time, her sister does not scatter.

Maureen walks to the bed, sits on its edge, close to Joan. She pries the bottle from Joan's grip, sets it on the carpet. When she feels her sister's body there, Joan turns onto her side, curling into her from behind like a caterpillar to a finger, as if by instinct. Maureen breathes a heavy sigh, sinks lower into her posture. Then, they're leaning into one another, Mo's elbow to Joan's hip.

I called you, you know. Lots of times, Maureen says, gaze ahead, away from Joan.

I know, Mo. I know.

It really fucked me up when you left like that.

You seem fine to me, Maureen. Same as always.

Joan, it's only that I stayed all this time. And you … didn't.

Nothing I ever did was good enough.

And everything I did seemed better than it really was. Ma was a difficult woman.

At least you stuck it out.

I'm not perfect like you seem to think I am. I've had my struggles, same as all of us.

Oh yeah? Like what, Joan says, propping herself up on an elbow.

Well, let's see, Maureen says, counting each failure on a finger. A marriage that's near fallen apart, a job that's near dead-end, a lack of friends … should I go on?

I don't know why she didn't give the house to you.

Maureen reaches toward the nightstand then. A small wooden box is latched shut. She picks up the box, sets it on her lap. I remember this, she says. Then, carefully, she lifts the lid. Inside, on a delicate gold chain, hangs a pendant. Maureen cups her palm around the necklace like a nest surrounds an egg. Then, she fishes for the chain hanging around her own neck, drawing it out from under the collar of her shirt. Joan sees her own name etched into the other heart's half, set against Maureen's chest.

Remember, she got these for us all those years ago? I think it's clear what Ma wants, what she's always wanted, Maureen says, holding Joan's half of the heart toward her. Seems to me like she just wants us to be together.

Joan sits up to take the necklace from Maureen, sliding it into the front breast pocket of her black leather jacket. She pats her heart and grabs for the bottle. Standing then, she looks down on Maureen. Let's get out of this room, Joan says.

Maureen stalls. Tomorrow's going to be tough, she says.

Joan notices how Maureen looks around the room, as though for a moment, she's forgotten where she is. Maureen's need or ... some kind of absence in her eyes seems to discomfort them both. Then, without a thought, Joan says, At least we'll have each other. Suddenly, she's uneasy, as if a hairpin turn lies ahead and she's cut the corner too close.

Unlit cig on the ready, Joan's in the kitchen. Takes a glass from the cabinet, loads it with ice. Pours, then downs another whiskey. She opens the fridge, rifling through old condiments like she's searching for something. When the refrigerator door shuts, she stands hands to hips, like a triangle, so she won't tip over. Her chest hollows when she breathes long. Drained, she says to the room, How are we supposed to get through this tomorrow, Ma?

Then, on the fridge door, she notices one magnet Ma mounted there as long ago as Joan can remember. From that same trip to Battle Beach they'd taken in the old station wagon. Painted on the magnet, the black sand beach that Maureen and Joan ran barefoot on in the rain together. In cursive writing it says: *Happiness Comes in Waves.* Tucked behind the magnet, a list. Joan tugs at the paper. A grocery list from a couple weeks back in Ma's handwriting. She wrote the date small on its corner. Joan's throat tightens when she reads the first line: *Fish & Flowers from Pike,* as if Ma knew what was coming, that both girls would somehow be here for Sunday dinner soon enough, all three, together.

Maureen, where are you? Joan shouts. I need you here, in the kitchen.

What's wrong? Maureen asks, rushing into the room.

Look, Joan says, holding the note toward her.

What … what's that?

Well, Mo, it looks like Ma's sending us on errands from fucking heaven. Then, she checks the top of the fridge. Ma's old blue vase has now been replaced by a larger one—clear glass and clean, like new. How Joan moves for the thing is like a reflex, even after all this time. She sets the empty vase on the table, a habit that's banked in her body's memory, way down, in its deepest vault. Suddenly, Joan says, Let's get out of here, as if turning a key. We're going to Pike for Ma, she says. I need to walk, she says as if she's been freed.

Just when she feels like she's coming down, there's that uphill battle toward Pike. If any city can unravel and subdue her, it's Seattle, with its noise and raucous traffic, its street vendors and edgy volatile panhandlers … distractions. They step around puddles left over from daytime rain and a dark corner beckons Joan's attention, sea air mixing with the sour stench of piss wafting from the stoop of the back entrance of an Asian restaurant. A heaped homeless woman, swaddled in wool, seems to have passed out in wait for late afternoon scraps.

A motor scooter swoops past them, swerving around a pothole. Maureen ducks under a flowerpot hanging from a trellis overhead in the alley shortcut they've taken. They've emerged onto Second Avenue at the end of the alley, and Joan has to swing her arms hard to push her bulk up the street. There's more life up here, more noise.

It's not so bad here, Joan says, eyes straight ahead on the traffic. I forgot how good it feels to roam this city, I mean.

Maureen pushes ahead of Joan, dodging around a spare-changer holding a plastic cup out. It's changed a lot since you've been gone, she says.

They're stopped at a crosswalk. A flock of gulls, bright but looming, closes in on the women, then veers away sharply, squawking. Joan lights a cigarette. Drags hard and inhales to her core. Pulling a flask from her inside jacket pocket, she says, I'm sorry about the house, Maureen, and takes a drink.

I'm not, says Maureen.

What? You're not?

It's her way of saying sorry. She still wants you to come home. Always did.

And you? Joan asks. What do you want?

I want us to start from here.

After all this time?

This is still your home.

So just move on, you're saying. Just like that? Joan snaps her fingers.

After all this time, seems like the only way.

Joan's looking down at her feet when the light changes. Joan, Maureen says, elbowing her sister, light's green. On the other side of the street, there's Pike Place Market, just like she remembers it.

Do you remember when Ma used to take us here? Maureen says, then dashes forward into the market area.

All those afternoons she'd take her girls to Pike, when they'd run through the aisles of the market together while Ma picked up fish for Sunday dinner and flowers for the table if her garden couldn't provide. All those games of hide-and-seek, in and out of Pike's hidden crannies.

Joan flicks her cigarette into the street, then takes off following Maureen. Suddenly, she feels that rush like being shot into the veins of Seattle—just in time for the streets to start filling in around the market with fidgeting tourists like canned sardines. Joan scans the crowd for Maureen. But all she sees is a cityscape in random gaudy patches stitched together, then ripped back down at the seams, a city frayed at all edges. Where's her sister? A thick scent of old oil and chili spices swirls with espresso, clouding her. She rubs her eyes. A skateboard crew of grungy street kids nearly clips a bike messenger moving toward her.

Joan stumbles and spins around. Maureen? her voice is terse, sharp, and then, *Maureen?* She's yelling now.

Market crowds gush around her blurring into waves. But no Maureen. Joan shoulders through the market, dodging endless buckets lining endless stalls of floral artists. Booths with sunflowers and moss roses, flowers tossed together in reckless arrangements like a pizza, way up in the air, fragrant. She runs, hipping through all those rustic bouquets, each a little snitch of art slipped into a paper sack with a knot of burlap twine ... you know them well from all those times you came here as a kid. Little Joan, you were almost always the hider, and when Maureen couldn't find you, she'd panic until you jumped out from behind some artisan's booth all smiles and yelled, I got you! Now, Joan stalls at the end of one aisle, looks left, darts right. No Maureen. Back then, each of you had learned the reactions of the other like a needle knows grooves on vinyl. Pike's where you learned to find each other until, over time, you didn't need to look to know how to play; it became an ingrained sense. Now she skids to a stop, out of breath, bending forward with her hands on her knees. *Think, think.* Then you see the aisle you remember most.

Joan takes off again, shooting around the corner at the end, and there stands Maureen. In front of Ma's favorite fish stand. With a bouquet of flowers already cradled in the crook of her arm.

Maureen smiles—proud—and says, Well Joan, looks like this time, I got *you*.

For fuck's sake, Maureen, Joan says through the relieved smile that's dawned across her face. Beat, she fingers through her sweaty hair, fastening it back in place. Let's go home, she says.

From there, Joan drags her kid-sister along without ever touching her, sailing downhill through Seattle with the stink of salmon under her own arm and the sweetness of lilies under Maureen's.

♛

Back in the kitchen, Maureen drapes the strap of Ma's old apron over her neck, tying the strap behind her. She's already stemmed Ma's flowers; now, she's cleaning the fish for the reception tomorrow. Meanwhile, Joan pours herself a whiskey on the rocks.

You're supposed to leave tomorrow then? Maureen asks. After the reception, right?

Yes, I am. I mean I'm supposed to.

Have you decided what you're going to do about the house?

Joan looks straight into her sister's eyes. Well, the first thing we're going to do, she says, is replace that shitty front porch.

We? Maureen asks.

Yeah, we.

So you're staying?

We've got some things to figure out here, Joan says.

Alright then, she says, straight. But Joan notices Maureen's mouth turning up at each corner, like when she was only tall enough for Ma's notch on your bedroom door.

Are you okay here? Joan says. I just have to go and do something.

Joan heaves herself up the stairs with the backpack she'd brought. She brings the bottle of whiskey with her. In the dusky light of Ma's bedroom, she fumbles toward her mother's makeup mirror, where a ring of dust has gathered thick around the metal base. She flicks the switch, watches the glow ease across the cracked mahogany dresser. And there's an old snapshot: Maureen, Joan, and Ma, arms locked. She holds a nail clipper from the dresser up to her face. A fine sliver of Ma's fingernail dangles from the trimmer, as alive as her own breath.

Joan follows Ma's fingernail as it helicopters to the dresser, landing atop a card of some kind. What's that? She cups one eye. The death tarot card with a butterfly through the skull's crown. From that deck on the mantel. And on top of the card, a small box.

Inside she finds two tiny envelopes, one for each girl with their names written on the front in blurry cursive lettering. Ma's handwriting? Joan squints, narrows in. Opens Maureen's envelope and there they are, all of her sister's baby teeth. The ones Joan replaced with dollar bills after she'd been appointed tooth fairy by Ma. Joan figured out early on that Ma was really her fairy, so she became Maureen's. Joan loved watching Maureen's face light up when she lifted the pillow. Then she would shine, too, running over to Ma with Mo's tooth in hand and whisper to her mother, Got her again, Ma. Each tooth, for both girls. Ma had saved them all.

Bottle's closer to empty now. She swigs, moves to her mother's closet. There it hangs, Ma's fuchsia terry cloth robe she remembers most. Joan pictures Ma in the robe, perched on her green corduroy recliner, barely filling in the divot made over time. Joan wraps the robe around her. Ties a bow at the middle and stuffs one hand deep down its pocket. Swathed in pink, she holds her bottle in the other hand and slips her bare feet into the black spiked heels she'd brought. On tiptoes, she twirls like a dizzy ballerina.

♛

At sunrise, Joan wakes to Maureen's shadow looming over her. A cool spot on her cheek. Joan is softened by sleep, still fetal while day-old sour breath folds into her mother's tender scent of flowers and time. Joan squeezes the pillow tight and cracks her lips open.

Time to get moving, Joan, Maureen says. She pulls the drapes to one side, quietly, kindly. The air in the room is thin and frictionless.

Joan's still swaddled in Ma's robe. She sits on the edge of the bed, supported gently by her hands to either side. I must've passed out in this thing, she mutters, gazing down on her bare feet hovering just above the carpet. She's perched like a doll on a shelf, legs swaying back and forth. Ahead of her, strewn across the floor, are those spiked black heels she's supposed to squeeze into today for her mother's funeral. It's dark in here, she says.

I can see just fine, Maureen says. She walks to the mirror and touches the family photo lightly.

She walks toward Joan, reaching for her.

Right, Joan says, right. I'm up. I'm up. Maureen takes her hand back and Joan lifts herself out of the bed. She slips the robe off, clothed underneath. Standing in front of her sister, Joan folds the robe perfectly, without letting it fall, as if in procession. She passes the pink mound, like a lowered flag, from her hands to Maureen's.

I'll wait for you downstairs. We'll head out together, says Maureen. She brushes past Joan on her way through the bedroom door, electric in her leaving.

Joan hears Maureen's door shut from down the hall. She picks up the whiskey bottle from the floor next to the bed, sees a few good swigs left at the bottom. Twists the cap open. Stop. You're tired of this. You've had enough. She screws the cap back on. Tight. Tosses the bottle into the small trash bin beside Ma's bed. She wraps her arms around her front, sucks herself in, and stands taller. She rises. She brushes her teeth and disrobes. She lets warm water in the shower run over her hair, down her back. She soaps her skin softly, with care. Then, she puts on the dress she's brought and slides into her black high heels. Before leaving the room to join her sister, she stands against the window, forehead to the pane.

When the fog of her breath lifts off the glass, she swears she sees her again: Ma, crouched down low in her garden—chamomile, lilies, black-eyed Susans, and bleeding hearts—rampant amidst Seattle's October rain. Ma looks up toward the window, one hand holding down her straw hat, the other raised, waving a big broad stroke across the sky. Joan swears she sees her mother wink. She shudders. Shakes it off. Looks again. Ma's gone.

PUNISHED

SHE GIVES YOU very specific instructions. Do not divert, your wife said. It's your fifth anniversary, and this year, she gets to make the rules. The plan: You are to meet her at the far end of the hotel lobby bar under the chandelier at 8:00 p.m., sharp. She'll be waiting for you there. You are to wear your fanciest slacks—pressed and lint-free—with those Armani leather loafers she'd bought you last anniversary. Remember? She likes you in a white button-down dress shirt—no tie—open at the collar so she can see your bone. Shirt is to be tucked. Do not forget the belt, Remi. You choose the black one, leather. Then, you are to take a cab from your home in Highland Park all the way downtown—Michigan Avenue—to The Drake. Your cab's waiting in your driveway—just beyond the white picket fence—while you deadbolt the front door. There's enough food in the bowl to last for Kitty. Do not drive, she warned. You will not be coming home tonight.

Downtown, off the street, you're through the revolving door with snow on the tips of your loafers, the scent of ice and lake air on your skin. Somehow, you're reminded of clean sheets when the crisp of your chill hits the warm leather lobby. You take the scarf from around your neck. Undo your coat to drape over your arm. Wipe your feet while eyeing the room for her, nervous enough to feel the need to look busy. She said she'd be waiting for you. You check your watch. 8:10.

Where's the bar? you ask the front desk attendant. You think you recognize reservation in the demure woman's face—as if she knows something about you that you don't—when she turns her gaze toward her computer and points down the hall. You shift your scarf from one arm to the other. Thank you, you say, moving your head to catch her line of sight. She grins, redder in the cheeks than when you'd arrived.

Enjoy your stay, she says, eyes down.

Right, you say, wondering about her assumption that you were staying the night.

Toward the bar, the hallway is carpeted in plush maroon. Along the wall, framed photos—lake landscapes in black-and-white and candid street shots of Chicago city-goers. One woman behind the glass catches your eye because the photograph was taken from behind. You wonder how you can feel so much without being able to see her face.

With the bar just ahead, you walk slowly—with trepidation—shifting your coat from one arm to the other, your heart in a race to get to her, to make certain she's here. Plus, you're late, and she was very particular about you being on time for this date. Sharp, she'd said. Remember? Shit. Stalling, you run your fingers through your hair, smoothing down the back. These unknowns make your clothes feel tight. You unbutton one more at your collar, wave your hand at your face for air. Your wedding ring. She'd told you to remove it. Right. You struggle with the platinum band, hands swollen from unease. Finally, it's off, in the palm of your hand, then slid down the slim front pocket of your slacks. Suddenly, you imagine the young busty front desk attendant. You turn to look behind you, over your shoulder, toward her post. The hallway seems narrower down there. You shake your head with a fleeting thought about being late enough so your wife doesn't wait—what the young woman might agree to with you and your naked ring finger. Your scarf drops. Bending down, you notice the stains on your shoes—sleet and sidewalk salt. With the scarf's tassels, you wipe your loafers clean before continuing on.

There she is. Right where she said she'd be. Bar. Far end. Under the chandelier. You recognize your wife only by her long red hair gathered at her front. When you approach, she's twirling the bundle, combing the ends with her fingers. Then, she spreads the hair evenly along her front, her whole chest draped in a thick curly blaze. Her tight black dress has a lace collar held around her throat by a small button in the back. There's a slit down the back of the dress from her nape to her waist. A strip of her skin shows—like milk spilling down the length of her spine. You can't remember the last time you saw her in black. The wife you know loves color. When she shifts her slim body in the high-backed bar chair to lean into her elbows on the bar, her naked shoulder blades cradle the curve of her long backbone. You want to touch her. To run your finger over the small bone at the base of her neck, a pearl cushioned by the rippled shell of her clavicle. You know these unseen parts of her as only a husband would. Your mouth waters.

She's laughing lightly with the bartender when you slide into the seat next to her. There's an empty cocktail glass between her hands on the bar. She prods the bottom of the glass with her straw, flips her hair, then tucks a strand behind her ear. The bartender asks her if she wants another—Another Manhattan, Miss? he says, and she only grins, gazing at him. Then, with her fingers, she digs out the maraschino on its stem from the ice at the bottom of her glass. She tilts her head back under the dangling cherry, then drops the piece into her mouth and looks ahead.

Sorry I'm late, you say, situating your coat to drape over the back of the chair. Then, you reach over to touch her shoulder. When she leans away from you, your fingers are left to tremble, suspended like a fly to her nectar. I get it, you say. You're mad. I'm late.

Do I know you from somewhere? she asks you.

Very funny, honey. Look, there was traffic on the toll road, and then the cab ...

She swivels the chair to face you, uncrossing her bare legs. When she leans toward you, you're reminded of the first time you inhaled Chanel N°5 off her neck years back. The scent of your wife's skin taught you how to recognize the knockoff. The kind you'd come to find lingering on your coat the day after your one and only indiscretion involving another woman from the office. You knew right away it was not the real thing. The cheap one clung to your clothes, up your nose for days. Your wife's Chanel would blossom around her only when she was actually present in the room. Like when she'd lick her fingers and wave her wrist to turn the page of *The New Yorker* while across from you during breakfast in the nook against suburbs through bay windows. When the table was cleared and your wife was gone, there was never a trace of her to be found. Suddenly, you wonder about that one other woman and the knock-off—your infidelity. For an instant, you consider how things would be different if your wife had found you out.

Now, here, her scent—like a landmark—is your only reference point. Looking at her, you feel as if you're roaming an unknown city—down dark alleyways of her bare legs under thigh-high spiked heel boots, aside the architecture of her whole lean body under the fit of her dress. This woman is no sculpture you've seen before. How she's painted her face—blood-red lips and thick lines—makes you yearn for her, so you gather her whole face in your gaze. When you look into the glassy shards of her blue eyes, you're reminded of a weapon. You reach your hand toward the open space between her knees. She shuts her legs.

Honey? she says. Quite the presumption, calling me that on first sight.

Right, you laugh, we're playing now.

Is something funny? she asks.

Alright, darling, you say. But you're nervous, and you know she sees it. This foreign woman still knows you in ways only a wife would—like how your body moves when you're pretending. You smooth your hair back with both hands. Let's go to our room so I can properly wish you a happy anniversary, you whisper toward her.

I was married, once, she says. Not tonight.

Come on now, honey. What do you want me to say? She slaps you then. One terse rap on the back of your hand, against the knuckles. You look at her ring finger. Naked. Suddenly, you feel compelled to play along, as if you have no other choice. Okay, okay, you say. What happened?

He was a *very* bad boy. You stare at her—brow furrowed, mouth tight—as she continues. I think all men need to be punished, she says. She opens her legs wider. You sense her nakedness when she puts one hand to each of your kneecaps and digs her fingernails in. You lean back as she leans forward. She's close enough for you to smell the sour cherry of her cocktail on her tongue when she says, Do you want to get *punished*, Sir? You watch her mouth, the way she uses all of her parts when she speaks. How her mouth cloaks the stress of the word with a slipknot of motive—*punished*—how she pinches her pink tongue between white picket fence teeth—*pun-ished*—the way she folds the word along her gums—*punished*—her lips, skintight around the shape of those sounds—*punished*—a word decapitated by her perfect mouth at the end. A clean cut. She grins, and suddenly, you're throbbing.

Well? she says.

Yes, you say. Yes I do, darling. I do.

Tonight, you will call me Mistress. She takes a key card out from her purse, sets it on the bar. Do you understand?

Yes ... Mistress.

Room 1010. Wait exactly thirty minutes. Knock three times to be let in. She runs her hand through your hair. That scent of Chanel off her wrist unravels you. She twists your ear, pulls your head back, and says, Do you understand me?

Before you can answer, she's gone.

Tenth floor. You slide your hands down your pockets roaming the hallway to find the correct room. 1010. You check your watch. Right on time. Sweat from your palms is hot against your thighs through the fabric of your pressed slacks. At the door to the room, you stop. The top floor view will show you the lake, once you can manage to get yourself inside. You gaze down the hallway. There's an exit route—stairs to the roof—just up ahead beyond the room. Suddenly, you're desperate for more air, for city wind, for ice against your skin. You imagine the openness up there, how you'd step to the edge and look over. With shallow breath, you tug at your shirt, venting near the armpits, then untuck it from your beltline. Black leather. You'd remembered. Then, you draw a long breath in through your nostrils. You retain the breath—at the top of your lungs—as if it was your last. One. Knock. Beat. Your heart. Beat. Echo. Empty. Cavity. Your chest. Two. Knock. Beat. Exhale. Knock. BeatBeatBeat.

When your wife opens the door, your chin has dropped to your chest. You lift your head, slowly, gazing along the length of her, starting at her feet. Spiked heel boots have not been removed. One spike holds her weight while the other props the door. Long legs are bare, fair against black leather. Her sheen reminds you of snakeskin. She has removed her black dress from earlier. Black lace garters are fastened around the top of each thigh. Tiny bows on each belt excite you, and your arousal by bits of innocence feels like sin. Suddenly, your forehead is hot, your cheeks are hot, the nape of your neck—hot—your whole face burns. Attached to the garters—one wide strap of black. It runs across her sex and up her torso. At her ribs, the strap splits to cover each breast—situated over her nipples—but you can see the round of pigment you know so well, the skin that spreads beyond the strap's width, skin the color only a lover could describe—her whole chest unfettered, yet hidden. Then, your gaze inches along the length of her breastbone— her long ivory torso like a tusk—your mouth wet imagining the bareness hidden from you. Your slacks begin to constrict, as if your sex takes a breath of its own.

What is this? you say, and you're shifting from one foot to the other, trying to see behind her into the room. She situates her body to block your view—arms, chest stretched across the doorframe. Suddenly, you're angry. You try to dodge her. She does not move an inch. What is this? Her body—close enough to breathe her in— quells your exertion like a hydrant. Her power matures with the Chanel under latex on her skin. Move aside, you say, but you're meeker now, afraid to make eye-contact. What is this? Your body's hardening is uncontrollable. Its reaction—like a spasm—confuses you. You feel like the hunted with a hunger that gets you trapped. You do *not* want to like this.

Let me in, you say toward the floor, and you hear yourself whine like a frustrated child.

No talking, she says, spikes planted.

Just let me through, you say.

You will not speak unless spoken to.

Alright. Just let me in.

You will call me Mistress.

Let me in.

Do you understand?

Let me in, Mistress.

Look at me.

I can't.

You will.

I won't.

When she draws her arm out from behind her back, you clasp your hands behind you as if cuffed. You—hunch, rounding into yourself. She—broadens, more bullish than before. There's a leather riding crop in her hand. She runs the whip up your leg, along your inner thigh, to your hard middle. She continues. Slow, slow, slow, she crawls the keeper upward, along each buttonhole of your collared shirt. Just under your chin—SMACK—she stops, then forces your gaze toward her eyes. Your face is lifted like meat on a spatula. Your hands are kept clamped down on one another right where they are—behind you.

You will, she says.

The mask is a band of black. Her perfect lips—stained in red—are fuller in the absence of her wide eyes. You've always adored her wide blue eyes. Now, through the slits, she glares—blue eyes sharpened into little knives. Her long red hair is braided, resting along her front like a whip. You look beyond her toward the view.

On the lake—white winter light, like ice. White light on glass—ice. You shudder. She stands back—just slightly—away from you. The entire anonymous woman.

You take a full look. Her most private parts edited like words on the page of her body—slashed but legible—and in that last moment before you enter the room, it occurs to you just how fine the line really is. One line of latex—a flimsy belt—the only bar between the intimate and the exposed. Is this enough to keep you out of her? No one else is here to stop all this, to stop you from devouring her with desire as your authority. Your distress can't stop this. If you lunge at her, would she stop this? (You're *desperate* to stop this.) You close your eyes. Stop this, you say, imagining your modest wife—floral prints at the kitchen sink, dish soap on her hands. Open eyes—a nameless Mistress. Your abdomen aches for her.

May I enter, Mistress? you say, and you don't recognize your own deep voice—weaker and restrained. All control is lost. Your appetite for her—your *curiosity*—moves you across the threshold. Afflicted.

DO NOT DISTURB. She deadbolts the door.

Stand there, she points to the edge of the bed. Do not move.

This room has high ceilings. The bed is king, made perfectly with white down, white pillows. When she walks toward the windows, you notice how her strap is flossed around her backside. She draws the heavy blinds. White light is thickened by the dark. You feel heavy on your feet when she turns toward you to approach. Carefully, she lays her whip on the bed. Then, she moves behind you, reaching around to your front. She runs her hands down your chest, unbuttoning along the way.

Wait, you say. Let me look at you, Mistress.

No talking, she says, then pinches the tender skin around your nipple. She removes your shirt. She runs her hands along your front toward your groin. You squeeze your legs, afraid her touch will ruin you completely. Her hands are cupped around you when she breathes into your ear. Then, she turns you around, to face her. Unbuckles your black leather belt, zipper, boxers. Step out, she says, and you know she means from your remaining clothes. She unthreads the belt from your slacks. Naked, you shiver—eyes on the windows wishing for that icy view—your hands covering yourself. She kicks your clothes to the side.

Yes, Mistress.

Bed, she says. Facedown.

Yes, Mistress.

You recognize your belt lashed against your backside by its smell of leather over your own scent. Whipped by your own belonging, you squirm, angry. What the fuck?

Now, now, she says, and spanks you again.

Stop this.

Turn over.

Stop it right now, you say, but you don't try to get up. Instead, you do as you're told. You flip over shyly, trying to cover your parts with a pillow, as if she's never seen your body before.

You're on your back now, and there she is, above you. Propped by your elbows—your sex like a saber—all you want is to take her. She unties the strap at her neck. You watch while the lines across her body are erased. She holds the strap taut between her two fists. Then, she comes to you, climbs on top, her knees to either side of your hips. You bring your hands toward her ribs, to try to touch her, but she wedges each wrist under a knee—her weight, the only restraint. It's enough. You lie back. Somehow, her power is enough. Enough to constrain you. She leans forward, her full bare chest aimed at your face. She lifts one knee to remove your limb from under her, then takes your hand, guides your arm above your head. You suck your stomach in when she fastens one wrist to the frame of the bed. Now, the other arm—bound. Then, you're widened— chest spread along the width of the bed—and you look at your own body, gazing side-to-side, following the breadth of your chest, along the muscles of your arms spanned like wings, and you think … you think, somehow, you feel beautiful like this. When you look at her then, you grin, softly, softer than you can ever remember. She shifts her head, sits back on you. She breathes. You shift your middle up toward her, your intent—to be inside her. But she rears. She's on both knees. She situates the black strap over your eyes. So tight—too tight—she ties. It's time, she says, and in the darkness of your mind—on the cross—you are no longer beautiful. You're blind.

A knock. You hear your Mistress walk to the door. Who's here? you say, and you cross your legs trying to hide yourself. Who is that? you say with invisible aim, Is someone else here? Silence. The whip against your thigh. No talking.

The other woman comes to you. You smell her youth when she's close—a harmless scent of sweet cherries and lime. She touches you. Cool skin from the air outside. You feel her on the bed. She spreads herself on top of you. What? you say. No, no, get off of me, you say, and you shift your bottom half. Where is she? Where's my wife? you say, but the other woman has you pinned. When she rubs herself along your front, you feel the prime of her tight chest, this woman, this younger woman's scent, the sweetness of her breath— you're dying for her … you're dying for her to STOP—she licks you from groin to throat.

You've slipped inside her.

She tightens.

You crack.

She flexes.

You moan.

She shifts.

You shatter.

You're coming.

You can't hold your body together.

I'M GOING TO EXPLODE! you yell, and you think of your wife—the real thing—simple and floral, and you're crying, you're crying now when you say, Please, I don't want to come. I don't want to come, you say. Please! You thrash your head from side-to-side. You hate them—this other woman and your Mistress. The blindfold has come down slightly from one of your eyes. You're still inside her, and you're yelling, Please don't make me come! but she's moving faster now, so you bite your bottom lip. You try to catch a glimpse of the other woman. You do. The front desk attendant rides you like a bull. No. You bite yourself harder. Blood. Iron. You hate yourself with a raging fire—for your infidelity now, for every indiscretion of the past. Punished.

Finally, you hear her. It's your wife's voice—your Mistress—from somewhere across the room. Next time you find your way to another woman, she says, I will say how. I will say who. I will say when. Do you understand?

Yes, Mistress, you say, while the attendant kisses your mouth.

Go on then, she says to the front desk attendant.

Yes, you moan, yes, yes.

Finish him.

Finished.

In the morning, she's left you a note. You are to meet her in the hotel café for coffee and a nice scone. *Don't be late, honey!* Your wife is nowhere to be found. Thick blinds are now pulled back. Yellow light off the lake warms you through the glass. Defeated, you run your finger across the window. Ice makes water out there, on the sill, in the sun.

Downstairs, you look for her in the café. There she is. Far table, near the windows facing Michigan Avenue. She doesn't see you when you look her over from a distance. Her hair is pulled back into a tight bun. The collar of her floral blouse is high-necked, covering her entire chest. Her shirt is tucked into jeans, and on her feet—simple sneakers, white with laces. She's got a scarf around her shoulders, and she sets her spoon down perfectly after stirring sugar into her coffee. You take a long breath and straighten before you approach.

Morning, you say.

Morning, she replies, face sheltered by her menu. She shifts her glasses on her face. I'm thinking Eggs Benedict, she says, eyes down.

Yes, you say. Great. Good. Thanks, by the way.

For what? she asks.

The scone.

Right.

Great.

Good.

You slide down in your seat, bring the menu up in front of you. Over its edge, you're sneaking glances at her. Her eyes are plain now—magnified by her glasses—natural and wide like a trusting child. Suddenly, she moves her eyes toward you. Quickly, you look down. Then back up. But her eyes are down again, and neither of you seem able. Eggs Benedict? you ask, staring at your lap.

Right, she says.

Great.

Good.

When the waiter comes to take your order, your wife gives hers while you look beyond the café to the lobby. At the front desk, there she is—the other woman—now in uniform as you'd seen her just yesterday. A sharp breath up your nose and you hold, moving your menu up to cover your line of sight so your wife can't see you look. Immediately, you ache. You look at your wife, still ordering. Then back again, at the other woman. The attendant catches your glance just as you're about to look away again. She grins. Shakes her head, looks down again.

Remi, your wife says, *Speak*. She nudges your leg with her foot under the table.

Speak?

Your order.

Yes ... dear.

Right.

Great.

Good.

READING GUIDE

The purpose of *MONARCH* is to animate the human experience of internal change against the outer landscape of America where social justice issues act as catalysts. Cycles of life, death, and rebirth are scaffolding for the narrative journeys. Some cycles are deeply transformative, others subtle. While the issues faced vary, all characters share an ability to change in relation to their wounds, as they encounter harrowing, transformative obstacles. In this, each character reigns as sovereign, traversing the bridge between thematic poles.

The following guide offers support to readers as they follow characters who often suffer before they transform These prompts are intended to inspire discourse so that readers, writers, students, and creators of all kinds can experience empathy, compassion, and understanding. Through connection and exchange over the material, my hope is that seeds are planted, new works grow, and unity is harvested. I encourage all to emote freely in the space of safety *MONARCH*'s landscape provides.

♕

LIFE | Loss & Love

What will come is sure to go. What is love? Faceless, yet familiar. Formless, it slips through fingers like water. Limitless, whether fleeting or forever. Love is power expressed as small acts of kindness, heroism, and sacrifice. What can love do? Love can possess and pursue. Love hurts. Love heals. Love leaves, then comes to the rescue. In essence, *MONARCH* is a collection of love stories, yet each character faces loss in reckoning with love's power to transform.

In "**Monarch**," Georgia faces her shame, forever changed by Gabriel's love through the small act of buying her a sundae.

ꝳ How has committing a small act of kindness changed you? Write what might have happened as a chain reaction.

In "**Vida**," Wiley sacrifices her own needs in order to free her first love.

ꝳ Who have you loved that left? Write the ending to a love story in your life that ended too soon.

In "**Mouth Organ**," letting go is Bunny's great act of love for her son.

ꝳ What did your mother sacrifice for you? Write a letter in her voice to yourself as a young child.

DEATH | Suffering & Surrender

What is born is sure to die. Can death dawn and life go on? Death knocks on obscure doors. *MONARCH* deals with the demise of the body and beyond. Here, death can mean the erosion of identity, a reshaping of values, or crossing over from one state of being to another. Surrender is the prerequisite for these transformative deaths. Sometimes silent, other times expressive, haunting, or sudden, these pivotal moments light fires within and incite change. Through pain, healing happens, but only when old skin sheds.

In **"Under Her Cellophane Skin,"** Seattle streets are home to Lemon, a teenage runaway suffering from drug addiction who receives help from Art, her anonymous hero.

   ♞ Who are your anonymous heroes? Write the story of how they found you.

In **"Jesus Wears Bermudas,"** Faith experiences surrender through sharing her deepest buried trauma for the first time. In this bond, love transforms trauma into treasure.

   ♞ Where in your body is your deepest trauma buried? Write the story of a chance encounter that unlocks your chest.

In **"Lucky Penny,"** memories inspired by music help bring Penny to face her pain and surrender during a manic bipolar episode.

   ♞ Crack the safe of your memory bank with music that activates deep imagining. Find a song that reminds you of a past pain, hurt, or loss and freewrite from that space.

REBIRTH | Chrysalis & Change

What dies is sure to go on and fly. Is there life after death? *MONARCH* involves the remarkable human tendency toward resilience even when destroyed, destitute, and damaged. In the chrysalis, cracked hearts like fine china are salvaged, then pieced back together. Characters must return home to who they were before breaking free into someone new. Then, from womb to world, courage bears the trip for yet another cycle around the sun.

In **"Fish and Flowers,"** a mother's death brings two estranged sisters together, as Joan's childhood home becomes the space where she reckons with the past to finally find forgiveness.

 ⮞ Locate an old family photo or childhood relic passed down. Write a story from the perspective of the photographer or the giver.

In **"Red Cardboard Hearts Hanging From Strings,"** Liza's dream about a past love helps her awaken into a new version of herself.

 ⮞ How have your dreams helped you wake up? Who has died within you for a new version of yourself to be reborn? Write a love letter to the old you as the dreamer you are now.

In **"Nova,"** the car is chrysalis, a safe place where Bettie and Jones share their dark sides. From this home, they are born into a new bond and emerge, united as one for life.

 ⮞ Where has your deepest bonding taken place? How are you different now than when you began? Write a story that follows the narrative arc from entrance to emergence.

ACKNOWLEDGMENTS

This book was only possible through the spirits of multiple communities. Thank you to my literary community. To Chris Abani, thank you for helping me reclaim my power and learn to honor my own process of discovery. To my other mentors, Cate Kennedy, Claire Davis, and Valerie Laken, your support changed me, and I carry your teachings with me always. To the MFA program at Pacific University Oregon, my cohort, alumni, and all staff, to those I've been fortunate enough to cross paths with for mere moments and to those I've held onto since, thank you. Infinite gratitude to Black Lawrence Press and Nomadic Press along with Michaela Mullin, my soulful editor turned dearest friend. Thank you to my recovery community and my soul tribe. I am forever grateful for the villages.

And to the handful within the village who hover closest, this book was only born by you in constant care of my heart. Thank you, Mom and Dads—no three have loved me harder or longer. To my dearest Mama, you keep my heart hemmed in. Thank you for always helping me put my pieces back together. Dad, thank you for saving your own life so you could save mine. You are my pillar of patience. To my sponsor, Jacky, who has held the torch for me and countless others all these years—I love you, family. To V, my best one, who reminds me that NM when it matters most, thank you for teaching me what loyalty means under your wing. You are my Jones. To you, Maddie, for all these years of becoming tougher together always through it all. To a bold, brilliant scientist who has taught me more about love than logic, thank you for always reminding me that I am able. Thank you, Gramma, for showing me that love is not bound by time, space, or form. Your guidance gets me through.

Lastly, to all those who loved me and left me, hurt me and helped me, thank you for the stories. May this book be an offering of gratitude to the sufferers and survivors in all of us, and to love and truth as the bridge between.

Special appreciation goes out to the following publications that were homes to some of *MONARCH*'s stories:

Big Muddy, Vol. 22/23, 2023: "Red Cardboard Hearts Hanging from Strings" (Third Print).

Flying South, Vol. 6, 2019: "Red Cardboard Hearts Hanging from Strings" (First Print).

Furrow, Vol. 15, Issue 1, 2014: "What My Momma Knows Is True."

Jerry Jazz Musician, Short Fiction Contest Winner 2021 / Pushcart Prize Nominee, 2022: "Mouth Organ."

The Ocotillo Review, Vol. 5.2, 2021: "Punished."

The Opiate, Vol. 24, 2021: "Nova."

Peauxdunque Review, Vol. 1, Issue 9, 2023: "Fish and Flowers."

Santa Clara Review, Vol. 107, Issue 2, 2020: "Paper Cranes" (retitled "Red Cardboard Hearts Hanging from Strings").

Spoon Knife, Vol. 7, 2023: "Vida."

Tahoma Literary Review, Issue 23, 2022: "Jesus Wears Bermudas."

Talking River Review, Issue 46, 2018: "Run" (retitled "Nova"), (First Print).

TulipTree Review, Spring/Summer Wild Women Issue 11, 2022: "Monarch."

Typehouse, Vol. 9, Issue 24, 2022: "Under Her Cellophane Skin."

EMILY JON TOBIAS is an American author and poet. She is an award-winning writer whose work has been nominated for the Pushcart Prize, along with other honorable mentions, and has been featured in various literary journals and magazines. She holds a Master of Fine Arts in Writing from Pacific University Oregon. *MONARCH: Stories* (Black Lawrence Press, 2024) is her debut collection. Midwestern-raised, she now lives and writes on the coast of Southern California.